Bound by Dragonsfyre

Bound by Dragonsfyre

by

Julia Phillips Smith

Editor Debra L. Stang, http://www.debrastang.net/

Cover design by Andrew Miller

Interior design by Hale Author Services

Stare of the Dragon watercolor ink print by Paulette Phillips, used by permission

ISBN 978-0-9878203-1-0

DEDICATION

Words can grant life or bring down governments, yet words are paltry things when called upon to translate emotion into intellectual conceit.

Words will never do justice for your cherished place in my heart, Brad.

Until they do, this book is for you.

Acknowledgments

As I will do with each book, I want to thank my husband Brad. His belief in me steadies and supports like the immutable laws of the universe.

To the White Point Beach brainstorming troika: working together has been a high point in my creative life. Thank you to Tara MacDonald and Shawna Romkey for helping to steer this story toward the finish line.

I would like to thank several groups of critique readers whose feedback shaped this book:

To the online readers of the serialized fiction version of this story, posted between April 2, 2010 and May 9, 2012 on my blog, A Piece of My Mind — your expectation of a new installment each week gave this story its heart. In particular I want to thank Grandma @ Grandma's Goulash and Alice Audrey @ AliceAudrey.com for hosting the serialized blog hubs, Weekend Writers Retreat and The Serialists, in which I was honored to take part.

To the dedicated commenters, your continued response to Scorpius and his adventures literally shaped this story into the novel it is today. My greatest thanks go to Alice Audrey and Travis Cody, who left comments for nearly every installment.

I also want to thank Ann Pino, Melissa Bradley, Janet Corcoran, Grandma @ Grandma's Goulash, Old Egg, Naquillity, Susan Helene Gottfried and A Kwee Life for supporting this tale and its author.

To my final critique readers: Travis Crowell, Tara MacDonald, Paulette Phillips, Connie Robinson and Caroline Ruyle for helping to polish the book into a lean, mean version.

To my editor, Debra L. Stang: for delving further still, you have my heartfelt thanks.

To my formatter, Michael Hale @ Hale Author Services:

your care and attention to this project is unsurpassed.

To my cover designer, Andrew Miller — for your patience and your continued enthusiasm for taking on these projects with me, my deepest gratitude.

A final thank you to my cover model, Bobby. You really nailed it.

Three Noble Houses from the Eighth Dominion

House of Tarsasag
>Lord Nizhnii
>Lord Zorjak

House of Razlava
>Duke of Razlava
>His heir, Lord Dirske
>His granddaughter, Lady Aerthrudha

House of Pruzhnino
>Duke of Pruzhnino
>His wife, the dukessa
>His heir, the markiisi
>His second son, Lord Thibault
>His eldest daughter, Lady Agridha
>His brother, Lord Visigard

ALSO BY JULIA PHILLIPS SMITH

Saint Sanguinus

1

The falconer strode silently ahead of him. Hurrying to keep pace, Scorpius kept sneaking looks back at the home he'd shared with the other fostered boys and girls until the road turned and there was nothing more to see.

His new master didn't bother to check to see if he was being followed. For one long moment, Scorpius stood in the road, unwilling to leave his hopes behind.

The distance stretched between himself and the falconer. All the moments when he'd shrugged away from Nurse's embrace, wished for quiet when the babies shrieked, or sighed with boredom during chores came rushing back. He'd take it all again gladly if only he didn't have to go with this dark-haired man clad head to foot in dark, worn leather.

In fact, those dark features had given Scorpius hope at first. Could it be, at long last, that someone from his family had come to fetch him from the nursery?

He gazed with longing at the turn that concealed the high stone wall and the manor where he'd grown to boyhood. Groomed to one day take his place among his noble house, Scorpius was now the only one left from his group of little lords and ladies.

Glancing ahead of him, the empty road cautioned *speed, speed.*

He could run.

He could run off into the wilds. The scraggly brush could conceal him. The rough boulders could cradle him.

Yet how long would it take before the work-hardened body of the falconer chased him down? Not long, Scorpius figured.

Scorpius listened, but he couldn't even hear the footsteps of the falconer against the gravelly road. Gaze roaming over the landscape, Scorpius felt the patient breath of unseen predators upon his neck. Just daring to glance up, he saw clouds and sky but no shadow marring the blue.

He knew what it felt like to see that dwarfing wingspan, to scramble for cover only to see his dear friend disappear in a screech of flame. His chest seized horribly with dread.

Scorpius ran, sickly sweat congealing along his spine. He ran till the sight of the scarred man ahead of him made his heart swell with relief. He caught up, his breath loud and ragged in the late morning air. Still the falconer walked, never turning his head to see who panted and puffed behind him.

Falling into step with his new master, Scorpius fought the urge to look back. What was there to see? Nurse no longer needed him, and the falconer had need of a boy. He'd best get it through his head that no one had come to claim him, and now no one ever would.

2

In some ways the falconer's home was not much different from the one Scorpius had left behind. Another form of a nursery, its fledglings would serve the nobility.

His new master showed him where he would eat, where he would sleep, where he would wash up. Scorpius nodded as he would have nodded to Nurse, acutely aware of Richolf's strength, of the scar that ran across a face that otherwise revealed little.

Richolf led him behind the house, a shy look of pride softening angular features as the two of them neared several long buildings. A dog loped up to the master who patted him absently.

Scorpius saw the hunched form of a hawk through a screen as it perched. Bells tinkled from the shadows. The hawk screeched as the dog caught up to Scorpius and sniffed his hand insistently.

Richolf moved past him, opening the door to enter the bird's domain. With smooth, assured movements, the falconer slipped a heavy leather gauntlet onto his left hand, holding it out until the bird stepped upon it. A few motions later, the hawk was secured to his master with long leather ties.

Scorpius followed Richolf past the line of buildings, each housing a single falcon. The dog pranced with growing excitement as they made their way to the meadow just beyond.

The master bid Scorpius to find a stick and hit the bushes framing the field. Scorpius couldn't imagine why he should do such a thing. Nor could he imagine questioning the order of a man who calmly held a ferocious bird at his command. He ran to the tree line, scrambled about for a stick, then glanced back at Richolf.

His master stood watching him, dark eyes watching with the same piercing gaze as the hawk. The dog half sat, half stood, ready to spring.

Scorpius turned back to the bushes, his skin crawling with

shame that he didn't know how to please this new master. He'd known everything that Nurse wanted or needed. He'd been able to anticipate what she'd want so that she'd smile so sweetly at him. Sometimes she'd even kissed the top of his head, or scooped him onto her lap and given him a squeeze, so that for a delicious instant, he'd melted into all her soft curves.

Thwacking the stick against the leaves like a ridiculous, overgrown babe, Scorpius' panic rose as he realized nothing whatsoever was happening. Richolf would be furious with him, he was sure of it.

Something flew directly at his face. His arms went up to shield himself as he turned away.

3

The game hen's feathers brushed his face as it beat its wings in furious effort. Scorpius saw his master release the hawk.

A part of him felt for the hen. Every shred of strength it possessed went into the fight to get away. The hawk flew in a different direction, gaining height. Circling back, it flapped its wings once, twice, gliding smoothly, apparently in no hurry at all. Even so, the distance between the hawk and the hen closed rapidly.

The kill was brief. One moment the game hen sped over the field. The next a startling collision knocked it from its flight path. The hawk carried it, dangling with wings askew, for several lengths before dropping it into the tall grasses. The dog raced to retrieve it and trotted in triumph to lay the prize at the master's feet.

Scorpius fought for breath as though he'd run for his own life. The hawk swooped low. Stretching the gloved arm out in welcome, Richolf settled the bird to his perch with a few bits of meat offered from a pouch around his waist.

Scorpius could see where the game hen had hidden until he'd forced it into the open with his awkward swipes. He stared down into the maze of branches, into the little haven he'd destroyed with his stick.

He could still feel the love of life that had driven the hen to try. He could even taste it when they sat down to eat later that evening. The roasted hen filled his mouth with joyous flavor. It was better than anything he'd ever eaten back at the manor. The dog licked its lips, waiting with keen eyes for the skin and the bits thrown by their master.

Scorpius had been a part of this, had helped to send the hen on its way so the hawk could dive with its lethal strike. The dog had done its part, the master had done his, and Scorpius the same. No bread he'd helped to knead, no roots he'd helped to scrape for Cook had ever tasted so sweet.

In the weeks that followed, Richolf showed him how to

clean out the mews where the hawks were housed, how to prepare the meat tidbits used in training the birds, how to beat the grasses as well as bushes to drive different game into the open. He showed Scorpius how to identify burrows and nests, taught him what commands were used to co-ordinate the dog's efforts and the hawks', and demonstrated how to pluck, to skin and to prepare roasts.

Sometimes upon first waking, Scorpius still expected Nurse to call for him. He listened for the clink and rattle of the breakfast cart, for the babble of the babies, until he rubbed his eyes and heard the click of the dog's claws upon the main room floor.

Then he got up from his bed and dressed quickly, running a comb through his unruly hair, not wanting the master to be after him.

Scorpius hadn't known how starved he'd been for purpose until Richolf came to claim him. It thrilled Scorpius to be an integral part of the hunt. Discovering where he fit into the scheme of things gave his world form and weight. The crushing realization that his family had not come for him quickly gave way to the drive to be the best falconer's boy his master could ever have imagined.

4

The first time they arrived on their mounts, Richolf told Scorpius to stay put with a quick motion of his hand. His master walked out to meet them, his customary stride replaced by bowed head and averted glances.

Scorpius couldn't help himself. He stole to the window, peering through the beveled glass until he could catch glimpses of the visitors.

Something squeezed in his chest when Richolf laced his fingers together and stooped, making a stirrup for the lord to dismount. His master scurried to help the others down and whistled sharply for the dog, which came at a bound. Richolf took hold of two halters and tied the beasts to hitching posts as the gentlemen stood talking and gesturing. Scorpius was glad Richolf hadn't called for him to help with the other two mounts. He'd never been this close to such animals before.

Even while hurrying to secure the mounts himself, even while avoiding direct speech to the visitors, Richolf somehow managed to be the host to these noble strangers. He loosened several saddlebags, balancing them over each shoulder, while the gentleman chuckled over a joke. He signaled to the dog and bowed to the men, sweeping an elegant hand toward the field where he'd brought Scorpius to train in the hunt.

In a few moments, the hunting party disappeared down the lane between the falcon mews. Scorpius' heartbeat quickened as he contemplated following them. The silence in the empty cottage unnerved him more than his master's reaction to an order disobeyed. The emptiness yawned around him now. A future consequence held no weight for him.

He stole from the cottage, slipping along the wall with the stealth he'd learned back at the manor house, always careful never to wake the babies. Slipping past the long buildings with their captive birds of prey, Scorpius kept Richolf and the gentlemen in sight. When he got to the corner of the last building, he crouched and watched past the rough shingles.

The hunters and his master walked through the tall grasses along the edge of the woods, until Scorpius was certain they'd move past his sightline. He rose from his crouch, just about to slink after them, when the gentlemen stopped and Richolf turned to put the saddlebags down. He held one arm extended, a dark hawk perched upon the heavy leather gauntlet.

Scorpius ducked back behind the corner of the mews, but not quickly enough.

When he peeked again at his master, both the dog and Richolf stared at his hiding place. Scorpius' stomach seized with dread.

5

Scrambling away, Scorpius ran back to the cottage as swiftly and silently as he could.

He burst into the empty house, turning this way and that, not knowing how long he must wait before his master returned. What were they doing now, those noblemen? Oh why, why had he revealed himself? He so longed to see what transpired at the hunt, needing to know what to do when Richolf ordered him to assist.

To that end, he found a spot where he could sit and watch the massive beasts hitched to the post at the far side of the yard. His gaze roamed over the halters laced intricately over their heads. Such workmanship in the glossy saddles, even on the blankets beneath them, glinting ornaments proclaiming the worth of the absent riders.

It took most of the day for the party to return. By then, Scorpius had scavenged for a few bites from Richolf's cupboard, though he had not been given leave to do so. The cottage grew dark, yet he did not know how to light the lamps.

Unease ran through his gut. The gentlemen were loud with drink, yet his master served them all with practiced patience. Finally mounted, with their braces of game tied to their saddles, the guests cantered off in a blast of triumph.

Richolf turned towards the cottage, his face drawn and weary. Scorpius left watching at the window, moving quickly to stand near his place at the table.

The door opened and his master entered. His expression was masked by the gloom until he lit the lamps and turned to his new apprentice. Scorpius bowed his head, not wishing to see.

Cupboard doors opened and shut. A dish was set down before Scorpius, roasted hen upon it, a hastily torn hunk of bread beside it. Risking a glance, he watched Richolf collapse onto his chair and dig into his own simple meal.

Sliding back to sit, Scorpius ate with perplexed relief. Richolf did not speak, merely chewed and swallowed, so tired that his eyes closed as he sat there smudged with dust. The dog lay at the master's feet, waiting for scraps which Richolf tossed now and then.

Once the food was gone, his master sat at the table, head propped on one hand till Scorpius thought he must be asleep. Taking up his dish and reaching for the other one, Scorpius froze when his master's eyes opened to pin him with his gaze.

"What did you think I meant when I motioned for you to stay?" Richolf asked.

Whisking the dishes across the room to the sideboard, Scorpius turned to face the question with the solid cabinet behind him for support. "I thought you meant to keep out of sight, sir."

Richolf thought for a moment before he straightened. "And how long do you suppose you were out there, watching us?"

"Not long, sir."

"Long enough." Richolf rose from the table, undoing the clasps on his heavy doublet. Stumbling towards bed, he shrugged out of it, saying, "If you could track me at all, that's no small thing."

6

Striking out for the pillar rock, Scorpius' ears strained for telltale signs but heard nothing. There was only the *shoosh-shoosh* of his steps through the grass and the persistent breeze whistling through branches.

A snap and crack from the trees to his left stopped him in his tracks. A rolling pebble from the boulders to his right made him whirl, pulse quickening. He burst into a run, putting some distance between himself and whatever it was, for how could he know whether it was Richolf?

The pillar rock beckoned in the distance, its tip visible over the hunched trees stunted by wind. Golden morning light taunted as Scorpius felt eyes upon him, and not just the gaze of his master who'd sent him out in order to track him.

It was Scorpius' task to locate his master before he made it to the pillar, but Scorpius knew he was being hunted by something else. Stopping once again to scan the forest lurking over his shoulder, he saw nothing but heard groaning trees rub and sway, which made the hair rise on the back of his neck.

Don't be a baby, he told himself, forcing his body to face the pillar. His heavy steps made enough noise for an entire hunting party. A drunken one, at that.

Smiling to himself at the thought, Scorpius almost didn't hear the subtle flapping overhead. The smell of it was on the wind, a smell that never really left him. He looked up.

It had already banked and was receding over the treetops.

Scorpius' blood ran cold. He froze for a split second, unable to breathe.

As though trapped in dream, he turned from the trees with their tempting shelter. He would be fleeing toward an inferno if the great creature opened its mouth and roared out its pleasure. He raced instead for the outcroppings among the rocky crag just ahead.

He ran without seeing, his ragged breath jabbing his chest. He dove beneath a rough ledge as though an unseen hand pulled him beneath it. Scorpius skidded into the shadows, only to hear a grunt as he slammed into a body.

Panic nearly drove him to scramble away.

Unnatural stillness gripped the forest as the dragon reappeared above the tips of the trees. Scorpius lay immobile, as did whoever lay beside him under the rock ledge.

There was nothing to do but hold his breath, flattening himself till he matched the rock, staring in horrified fascination as the creature glided closer. Scorpius shook, though his trembling made his teeth chatter. Surely the dragon would hear such a racket.

Two strong hands settled over his shoulders. One touch and Scorpius knew who it was under this ledge with him. He quieted as the enormous wingspan blocked everything from view, then left only clear sky in its wake.

Scorpius caught his breath, his master holding him steady. From a skewed vantage point he could see the pillar rock, recoiling in his mind from images of himself trying to reach it as he'd been ordered to do. When the dragon swooped low to settle itself upon the pillar, a gasp escaped him.

Leathery wings stretched and retracted. The long, narrow head shook back and forth. Then a blood-curdling screech sliced through the valley.

Richolf held him tighter, as though his master knew the terror of his memories, though Scorpius had never told him any of it. Sharp stones dug into his hip, but there was no question of adjusting position. The dragon's perch atop the rock gave it a perfect view, its exceptional sight geared toward detecting motion.

All morning and well past noon, the dragon kept them hostage under their ledge. It finally dove in a spectacular rush upon a forest titan, spearing the unfortunate animal with its sword-like claws. With three flaps of those hideous wings, the dragon with its writhing meal finally flew out of sight.

Richolf held him there as they waited for any sign that the creature would return. Scorpius felt safe with his master's hands grounding him. The strength that flowed into Scorpius kept the remembered screams of his nightmares from bubbling to the surface.

Late afternoon sun carved shadows across the valley when Richolf nudged Scorpius out from beneath the ledge. Shouldering his hunting bag, his master inhaled carefully, searching for any signs of the dragon that might carry on the wind.

With a quick jerk of the head, Richolf gave the order to strike out for their cottage. Scorpius filed in behind him, using every ounce of self-control to refrain from reaching for his master's hand.

8

Scorpius nearly ran for the cottage once he finished cleaning the mews out back. How could he stop himself from looking up, always up? It might be swooping down even now.

The falcons must be fed and attended to, however. The birds were not Richolf's but the nobles'. This cottage and their positions here were tied to the nearby estate as closely as the falcons were tethered to Richolf when he took them out for the hunt.

Rounding the corner, Scorpius pulled up short at the sight of three mounts grazing beneath the trees at the edge of the clearing. The last time a visiting hunting party had descended upon the cottage, his master had told him to keep out of sight. Scorpius resolved to make up for his previous error, even if that meant staying out here where he did not want to be.

It didn't help that raised voices from the cottage made the mounts' ears prick forward. Scorpius settled himself under a dense sweep of branches just as a tumble of men poured out through the door.

He choked back a gasp, not that anyone could have heard him over that ruckus. Two of the lords looked ready to kill each other, rolling over the dusty ground as if they weren't wearing velvets and brocade. A third nobleman hovered just out of range, sword drawn.

Scorpius' heartbeat slowed to an icy sludge as their fight rose in pitch. When Richolf appeared at the doorway, relief flared inside him, only to dash to bits when his master faltered and sank to his knees.

He almost betrayed himself. He almost parted the screen of leaves and branches, nearly clambered to his master's side. A strangled cry gurgled up from the throat of one of the fighters, and Scorpius crouched still and silent.

The third nobleman with the sword strode over to the victor, stretching his hand out to be clasped. The lord in blue regained his feet, taking weary steps away from his opponent as his companion's sword plunged neatly through the fallen man's ribcage.

Scorpius clamped a hand over his mouth. The disheveled lord made his way to Richolf, who remained kneeling and bowed low. Scorpius couldn't make out what was being said, only saw his master shake his head vigorously.

The sword-wielding lord, also in blue, closed in on his master. Scorpius bit down on his lip so hard it bled.

With a vicious kick, the lord sent Richolf sprawling in the dirt. He choked with it as a boot planted itself in the center of his back.

"Swear it," the fighting lord said.

His master coughed and spit. "I swear, my lord."

The boot kicked Richolf in the ribs. His master writhed but made no sound. With no further glance at the falconer or the body they'd left behind, the noblemen climbed into their saddles and cantered off.

Scrambling to his feet, Scorpius burst from his hiding place, hurling himself beside his master who turned his face away.

"Help me inside," was all he said.

Great drops of blood as big as Scorpius' palm smeared the floor. Richolf made his way to a chair. The other lay overturned beside the table.

"Fetch some water," he said, fumbling for the cloth around his neck, pressing it to his eye.

Scorpius stood there, his gaze unseeing. His pulse fluttered beneath his skin. How he wished Nurse could walk through the door and set things to rights.

He remembered the morning when Mirko had walked along the high stone wall. A boy from a well-placed family, he'd never paid heed to their watchers' threats or warnings. A slip, a fall and his head had split open. Nurse had always been there to sort through all the blood and push aside the crying.

Glancing at his master, Scorpius saw how quickly the neck cloth reddened.

There was a clay jug of water on the sideboard. He heaved it onto the table as Richolf mumbled something about thread. Scorpius entered his master's bed chamber, ignoring the strangeness of it, and didn't leave until he'd found the needle and thread in a drawer.

He held the looking glass as Richolf took up the grim task of sewing up his own wound. "One day you'll join us on the hunt," he said, carefully pulling the thread taut. Fresh blood trickled over his brow, winding down his cheek to drip from his jaw.

"I can't bring you along before you're ready. Dragons are one thing." Richolf's gaze left the looking glass and focused on Scorpius. "The nobles are quite another."

So many questions tangled themselves around Scorpius' tongue. He bit them all back, for his master did not offer anything more. Scrounging up cloths and a bucket, they worked at sopping up the blood from the floor.

The body of the nobleman in its rich brown brocade lay where it had fallen in the clearing before the cottage. Scorpius snuck glances at it, grateful to be this far away from the corpse.

Richolf gazed off now and then, listening. Scorpius didn't know if he should dread anyone arriving or be grateful to have the body claimed. Yet no one came. Not until the next morning.

This time, when Richolf made that abrupt gesture, Scorpius not only stayed behind in the empty cottage, he slipped into the shadows, even as he watched his master open the door to face them.

10

"My lord Zorjak," Richolf said, bowing deeply and elegantly.

"Richolf."

Scorpius watched them from his hiding place. They turned to regard the body of the slain nobleman in the clearing.

"Very sad affair, my lord."

"Yes, it is. Yes. Sad indeed."

The two men moved out of Scorpius' view. This time he resisted the urge to follow. At least the new lord in his brown brocade doublet didn't seem bent on striking his master. Yet the deadly fight between the nobles replayed itself in Scorpius' mind without mercy. Richolf had told him to stay put, and this time he knew why he must hug the shadows.

The men's voices buzzed in the distance. Still no shouting. Scorpius' own breath sounded loud to him in the quiet cottage, his mouth pressed close against the cabinet door.

Finally the lord strutted into the cottage, followed respectfully by Scorpius' master and the dog. Richolf gave a quick hand signal to the animal, which instantly lay down out of the way. It settled its head on its paws, though its eyes strayed to Scorpius' hiding place.

The nobleman paid no heed whatsoever to the falconer's dog. He allowed Richolf to draw a chair out for him, settled himself upon it and gazed over at Scorpius' master. "What do we do about it then, do you suppose?"

"May I offer you a drink, my lord?"

A slight nod sent Richolf to fetch a goblet and fill it with wine. Lord Zorjak took a long sip, then rubbed his forehead with pinching fingers.

"Might I suggest, my lord, and I know this may sound disturbing..."

The nobleman gazed wearily at the goblet. "This entire business makes the blood recoil in my veins."

Richolf nodded. "Well then, my lord, I encountered a great-horn not three days hence."

Lord Zorjak's fingers tightened around the goblet's bowl.

"If we leave the body close to where it was sighted, the dragon will fly off with a meal and the unfortunate lord will have suffered a gruesome hunting accident."

The nobleman lifted the goblet to stare for a long moment into its depths. With a quick swig he downed its contents and slammed the cup down hard upon the table.

"You think my brother deserves to be pecked to pieces as carrion?" he asked.

"I think my lord deserves a chance to survive his brother," Richolf answered.

Scorpius watched in confused fascination as tears spilled down the nobleman's face.

11

The nobleman would not leave, staying far into the night. His guard remained outside, speaking in low tones.

Scorpius had paid attention at first while his master spoke with Lord Zorjak. Richolf served wine, nodded, and gave an opinion from time to time.

It was so late. Scorpius couldn't keep his eyes open. Leaning his head against the cabinet door, he slid uneasily into sleep until the door unlatched under his weight and he tumbled cross-eyed onto the floor.

He'd nearly forgotten why he'd been squashed in there to begin with. The smell of wine hung heavily in the air, and his gaze lit upon the glossy boots of the lord beyond the table legs.

Scorpius looked up at Richolf, but his master ignored him. Fear shot through Scorpius' body, jolting him wide awake.

It couldn't be safe to sit out in the open like this. He rose into a crouch, where he could now see the top of the nobleman's head.

"A bloody insult," Lord Zorjak slurred. "Swanning about. He's not the only one from the House of Tarsasag who's gathered a force behind him, calling them admirers."

Scorpius crept forward over the stone floor, cool against his hands. His master had hidden him away in the cabinet when the men came. That was the safest place for Scorpius to be. He could almost feel the burning stare of the nobleman upon his back. It sent creeping shivers to grab at his neck, as though he'd already been caught out.

When he was nearly within reach of the open door, a goblet sailed over his head to clatter against the wall above the cabinet. Dark red wine splashed over Scorpius, dripping onto the floor, splattering the wall.

Richolf moved smoothly to retrieve the goblet, crouching to wipe up the red stains. His master's eyes were bright with alarm as he locked gazes with Scorpius. Richolf gave the slightest flick of his head toward the hiding place. Scorpius darted forward, folding himself into its airless embrace as Richolf wiped at the wall above.

The door clicked shut behind Scorpius as Richolf turned toward the drunken nobleman. "Does my lord require more wine?" he asked.

12

When the nobleman had finally drunk his fill, his chin tucking low on his chest, Richolf opened the door and motioned to the weary guard without. They filed inside, wordlessly lifting their master from the chair to settle him, insensible, on Richolf's bed.

With a loosening of neckcloths and buckles, Lord Zorjak's men found places around the falconer's table. Richolf fed them all, pouring ale this time as Scorpius watched through the woven panel screen that served as the cabinet's doors. His stomach growled, but his master had made no move to let him out of his sanctuary. Best stay put.

Eventually, it was decided that two of the guard would wrap the body and haul it towards the pillar rock. The others would wait for their master to restore himself. How odd that the men assigned to the more grisly task seemed relieved.

Scorpius stared intently at one of the guard in particular, pressing his eye close to the tiny holes so he could see better. Had Richolf failed to explain about the dragon?

The cabinet door cracked open without warning. A boiled root tumbled into the darkness beside him even as Scorpius' heart still leapt into his throat. The door shut and his view of the table was blocked entirely.

He listened as plans were agreed upon and the two groups collected their gear to make ready. Whoever stood before the cabinet did not budge. Scorpius sat in complete darkness, the scent of the root filling the tiny space. He felt about blindly until his fingers hit upon the cooled root skin, his guts rejoicing noisily.

Scorpius raised it to his mouth, his teeth sinking greedily into the rich flesh. He'd never been overly fond of this type of root before. Strange how an evening in a cabinet could change things so drastically.

Satisfied for the time being, and with nothing to see through the blocked peepholes, Scorpius curled onto his side and closed his eyes. When he woke again, Richolf was pulling him out of the hiding place.

The men were gone. Lord Zorjak was gone. The body no longer lay outside the cottage.

Scorpius stood blearily before the open cabinet door as Richolf crouched before him, eye to eye. He cupped one roughened palm against Scorpius' cheek, his tired gaze shining with pride. A warm happiness spread through Scorpius' chest.

His master chucked him on the head and stood. "Let's get this put away, now," he said, turning to the cups and dishes littering the table and sideboard. Yawning, Scorpius collected the bowls and stumbled for the wash basin.

13

The falcon fussed on his perch. Scorpius sighed sharply but carried on, ducking out of reach of the bird's wings as they beat the air in irritation. This was the third mews he'd cleaned today, with nine more waiting for him.

Refusing to settle down, the hawk instead beat its wings even faster, whipping up dust and feathers. Scorpius barked at it to calm down just as two men entered the small building.

Dressed down for hunting, they were nevertheless clad in handsomely-worked leather and finely-woven wool. Swords hung from their hips and jewels glinted from their fingers.

Dropping to one knee and bowing his head in the smooth motion he'd perfected, Scorpius said, "My lords," in a clear voice. *The nobles were just like the falcons*, Richolf had taught him. Handle with the deference they demanded, but show no fear if he wanted respect in return.

"Your master about?"

"Yes, sir." He stared at the lord's polished wine-red boots.

"Fetch him, then — there's a lad."

From the corner of his eye, Scorpius watched the nobleman move toward the bird. He bit down the words that wanted to warn him away from the already moody falcon. However, he'd been dismissed. There was nothing for it but to obey.

As he dashed through the door into the sunlight, the falcon screeched and the lord cursed.

His master's intention for the day had been to inventory and bundle the fur pelts he took to the estate for trade. Scorpius headed for the shed where the pelts were cured, but when he breathlessly rounded the doorway, the shed was empty.

A sinking feeling gripped his belly. The nobles hadn't given prior notice, but that wasn't so out of the ordinary. However, he felt certain they would not take the news well if he couldn't locate his master and they were denied their hunt.

Taking off at a run, he sped to the cottage, not expecting to find him there but hoping for it anyway. "Sir?" he called as he burst through the door. "Sir?"

An idea surfaced but he rejected it as he hurried back to the noblemen. He'd never been instructed in such a plan. It could make things worse.

Nonetheless, his mind worked quickly and boldly over all the preparations he'd need in order to lead the lords to the hunt on his own. He'd take the large red-tail. Scorpius had a good rapport with the bird. The noblemen would get a guaranteed kill.

When he re-entered the mews and saw Richolf gathering up the very bird he'd planned to use, he swallowed disappointment to focus instead on the relief that spread over him.

14

Scorpius sensed a movement behind him and turned.

One of the lords had followed him out to the tall reeds, where he was set to flush out the larger marsh birds. The noble smiled at Scorpius, his display at odds with the piercing expression in his eyes. Unnerved, Scorpius nearly dropped his stick.

"My lord," he said, no longer at liberty to turn his back, to search for the game. Keeping his head slightly bowed, he could still see his master out on the edge of the tree line, likewise speaking to the other hunter.

"This is where you find them, I suppose," the noble said, gazing around with disinterest.

"There's bound to be one or two, my lord." He didn't smell any spirits on the man's breath that would explain such odd behavior.

The noble closed in on Scorpius, coming uncomfortably close. Scorpius kept his gaze down, but his breathing shallowed. Without warning, the lord yanked the stick from his grasp and held it up for both to see.

"What would I have to do to coax them into the open myself?"

Scorpius fought the stammer that dragged at his tongue. "Y-you take swipes at the clumps of reeds there," he said, gesturing towards the nearest one.

The noble stood nose to nose with Scorpius for a terrible moment, the stick raised to strike. Scorpius didn't dare to look up, could only keep track of the stick from the corner of his eye, his heart beating fast.

At last the hunter turned, strode a few steps and swung with assurance toward the possible hiding place. "Ah, yes," he said, turning back toward Scorpius to swing again.

The blow struck the back of his head, and he ducked. The yelp that formed in his chest did not get past his lips.

The noble chuckled. "Guess it can get away from you," he said, again closing in until Scorpius could feel the noble's breath lifting his hair. Scorpius didn't answer other than to nod quickly.

"You seem a smart young chap."

His mind went blank. Yet he must hang onto his wits, even as his skin erupted in tiny bumps.

"How long have you been with the falconer?" the noble asked, his voice both mild and unsettling.

"Three years this summer, my lord."

"That would be the very time for which I have an interest."

The welt along the back of Scorpius' head burned and protested. He kept his eye on the stick.

"A smart boy like you wouldn't forget something like a dragon sighting. Surely not."

Scorpius' breath snagged in his lungs. His mind flashed back to when he'd first arrived here, when the lord was stabbed to death right in front of him, as he'd hidden in the bushes outside of Richolf's cottage. He nearly looked up into the lord's face.

15

No fear, he heard Richolf say in his mind. *Don't let them sense any fear.*

The hot line of pain across the back of his head distracted him. "No, my lord," he forced out, struggling to banish the shaking in his voice. "I would never forget something like that."

A quick glance across the field showed his master watching him, the other lord whispering something to Richolf. This noble before him still stood too close. What if he could see that Scorpius trembled?

"It is not your master's answers I'm interested in at the moment," the noble said.

Richolf had needed stitching up that day, when the nobles had fought. Scorpius remembered how the royal brother had stayed so very long at the table, drinking wine and shedding tears. And how Scorpius had been shut up in that cabinet for hours.

He mustn't say the wrong thing. They'd hurt Richolf before. And Richolf had kept Scorpius out of sight until the royal guard and the drunken brother had gone.

He had to keep it all straight in his mind. He couldn't get it wrong. The noble tightened his grip on the stick, his gloved hands veiling the power lurking beneath. Scorpius swallowed but did not flinch away. *Show no fear.*

"Were you serving the falconer when Lord Nizhnii disappeared?" the noble asked.

Scorpius' heart pounded and pounded. Surely the noble could hear it. "No, my lord."

"Where were you, then?"

"Still at the nursery, my lord." He had to pay attention, pay attention and remember. He had to tell Richolf exactly what he was telling the lord now.

"Can you describe Lord Nizhnii for me?"

The chilling image of Nizhnii's body seized up in a pool of congealed blood came clearly to him. "No, my lord."

"And Lord Zorjak?"

Scorpius shook his head, the memory of the imposing nobleman in tears never very far away. "I'm sorry, my lord."

"Are you?" the noble said, his lips nearly touching Scorpius' forehead. "Sorry?"

Scorpius nodded. "I have served many nobles since I came here, but never Lord Nizhnii. And not Lord Zorjak, my lord." He couldn't stop the shaking now. There was no way the nobleman could miss it.

The lord pressed the edge of the stick hard against Scorpius' cheek. "Are you a good boy for your master?"

"I try to be, my lord."

The nobleman laughed then. "Such a careful answer. A very good boy, indeed."

16

Richolf motioned for the hunt to continue. Signaling *message received*, Scorpius waited for the lord to stand aside, unable to continue his duties without causing offense. The burning welt along the back of his head still cautioned him to beware. So far, the noble had proven to be painfully unpredictable.

However, the remainder of the hunt proceeded with no further hitches. The red-tail bagged an impressive brace of game for the nobles, and the four of them returned to Richolf's cottage as though nothing out of the ordinary had surfaced.

When the noble who'd stayed with his master leaned in close and spoke privately with Richolf, Scorpius saw the falconer's hands freeze momentarily as he tied the brace to the horse's saddle.

When he turned from preparing the other lord's supplies to find Richolf approaching, Scorpius' breath caught in his chest at the haunted look on his master's face.

"I'll be going to the estate with their lordships," Richolf said in a normal tone of voice. "You must look after the birds and the dog until I return."

"Yes, sir." Scorpius watched as the nobles climbed astride their mounts, exchanging their own glances with one another. He looked up into Richolf's eyes.

The same dread Scorpius had seen in those guards' eyes now belonged to his master. "I may be gone for a while. If anyone comes for a hunt, you know what to do."

Scorpius nodded, his chest hollowing out beneath his ribs. He noticed his master packed nothing of his own, merely set out on foot behind the two nobles.

The dog started following but halted in its tracks at a signal from Richolf. Scorpius called it back, but it ignored him for a long moment.

Two nights passed before he heard the longed-for steps in the gravel outside the window. Scorpius leaped to his feet to burst through the door.

A stranger stood there, a servant in the plainest of tunics. He nearly removed his cap until he saw that it was a boy come to greet him. "This the falconer's cottage?" he asked.

Scorpius forced his head to nod.

"You're to come with me, then," the young man said, already turning and striding away.

"Wait!"

Scorpius turned to look at the cottage, feeling the absence of his master keenly. What of the falcons, tethered inside their mews? And the dog — what about him?

The servant stopped in the road, the habit of taking orders impossible to break. Yet he knew he was higher on the pecking order than Scorpius, so he didn't bother to hide his impatience.

When Scorpius insisted on seeing to the animals before he set out for the estate, the servant stretched out on a patch of grass, placing his cap over his face until Scorpius nudged him with his foot. Not so inclined to hurry back as he'd been earlier, the young man glared up at him and cursed.

It was a long, awkward walk to the estate. Scorpius kept an eye and an ear out for any sign of leathery wings above, and was appalled by the servant's complete lack of caution. As for the servant, once he figured out what made Scorpius scan the skyline, he spit derisively into the hedgerow.

The rooftop of the estate appeared in the distance not a moment too soon.

Dumping him at the first footfall upon the estate grounds, the servant hurried back to his tasks as though it were Scorpius' fault that his work was now behind schedule. Left to find his own way, Scorpius' steps slowed as his neck craned this way and that. His stomach tightened with dread as other estate servants gave him unwelcoming glances and the slaves scurried past without meeting his eye.

Whom should he ask about Richolf? Assuming that was the reason he'd been summoned here — that infuriating servant sent to fetch him hadn't been a lick of help.

Think for a moment, he told himself. *Stop. Get your bearings.*

Scorpius found an out of the way spot tucked against a wall in order to scout. He tracked the comings and goings on the estate grounds, noting the differences between lowlier servants and highly-placed ones. He rubbed his hair to smooth it down from the dusty journey. He swiped at smears on his breeches, and made sure all his lacings and buckles were fastened. Richolf would be well-known here, and the last thing Scorpius wanted was to dishonor his master among this lot.

Propelling himself forward, he made his way past the out-buildings and closed in on the entrance used by servants and slaves alike. Everyone moved at a brisk clip. Scorpius had to trot to avoid slamming into people.

The entrance led to a dim corridor, which he followed along with everyone who knew where they were going. Finally it opened into a receiving area, where deliveries were haggled over and masters barked at their charges.

Scorpius scanned the faces but Richolf was nowhere among them. A canny older man held him in his sights as he directed staff and signed for purchases. Surely he would know where his master could be found. He might at least know why Scorpius had been sent for.

Taking a steadying breath, Scorpius navigated his way across the room until he stood before the well-dressed servant. Remembering to bow smartly, Scorpius announced himself and inquired as to his master.

The older man passed his notebook and stylus to another youth who hurried off. Brilliant blue eyes that seemed as if they had seen everything there was to see gazed through Scorpius, raking his thoughts and fears until the hairs on his body stood on end. There was a glimmer of recognition in the head servant's manner, but Scorpius had never been to this estate before.

Calling another young servant over, the older man said, "Show him to the sick room," and turned away to the next request.

18

At first all he could make out was a heap of rags in the gloom. Scorpius moved forward to kneel beside his master huddled insensible beneath tattered blankets. "Sir? Sir," he said, but nothing got past Richolf's chattering teeth.

Looking back at the grim guard standing in the doorway, Scorpius' plea for help shriveled on his tongue. His master would not suffer any further indignities, and that included an apprentice that begged.

Scorpius rose to his feet and informed the guard he would return, using his most authoritative tone of voice. His heart swelled with pride when the man nodded and backed out of the way.

Striding purposefully, though he didn't know where he should start looking, nor for what, Scorpius made his way back to the courtyard and stood adrift, his heart heavy in his chest. Who had reduced his master to this state? What did they want from a falconer that was worth such suffering?

There would be no hope of securing a horse. Scorpius must locate some other form of transport — but what? Keeping track of all the deliveries back and forth through the estate yard gates, he narrowed down his options until he was haggling with the owner of a dog cart.

With all the bluster he could manage, Scorpius prodded the unsympathetic guard to help load the falconer into the cart. His feet dangled disgracefully over the sides. Scorpius used the same signals his master used with their hunting dog and could have kissed the sturdy animal hitched to the cart when it followed his command. Before long, they were away from the estate and on the road for the falconer's cottage.

When they were far enough away from prying eyes, Scorpius stopped the cart to bend low over his master. In the sunlight, the reality of the swelling mess of Richolf's face clawed at the breath in Scorpius' chest. It wasn't simply a fever that kept his master from recognizing his apprentice.

"You'll be home soon, sir," Scorpius said, more for his own benefit than anything else. He coaxed the dog to carry on, and they trundled their way slowly over the road, Richolf moaning whenever the cart lurched.

The sun was already tucked well below the horizon when they finally arrived at the falconer's cottage. As Scorpius tried to work out how he was going to get his master out of the cart and onto his bed, their hunting dog snarled and barked at the intruder on his turf. The cart dog stopped in his tracks and set up an answering clamor.

Shouting at both animals to quiet down, Scorpius discovered Richolf had regained consciousness.

A pain-singed gaze settled on Scorpius. "We're home, sir," he said.

"Dragon. Took him off."

"Pardon, sir?" A worm of dread pierced Scorpius' heart at the mention of the murdered noble those three years past.

"Dragon. Swear it."

"Dragon, sir," Scorpius repeated. "The dragon took him off."

His master drifted into oblivion, leaving Scorpius with the barking dogs, disturbing wounds to dress and the unwelcome answer to his question from that long ago Night of the Cupboard. He would never again wonder why those guards had been relieved to chase down a dragon, when the alternative made him long to look away.

He would be grateful that it had been Richolf to fetch him away from the nursery, and stop wondering what it might be like to serve at the estate, with all its fine lords and ladies with fatal hunting trips and secrets so dark his own master now fought back its shadows.

19

"Let's get you inside, sir," Scorpius said, pulling his master upright and out of the cart.

Richolf shook with effort and fever. Scorpius was too consumed with his wobbly attempt at support to give in to the fear that nipped at his heels. The falconer could not stand, and it was still a long way to get his master into bed.

Scorpius' body swayed and buckled as he cajoled, coaxed and commanded Richolf to keep moving. They had just managed to cross the threshold into the cottage when his master slipped from his grasp and crumpled to the floor.

Fighting to catch his breath in the gloom of nightfall, Scorpius gazed across the cottage at the bed that was too far away. Unnerving moans drifted up from the falconer, while the dogs continued their noisy quarrel outside. Crouching down beside his master, he laid a hand upon Richolf's back while gathering the wits that meant to desert him.

It seemed an age before he finally struck upon a plan. Hauling his master's pallet from the bed frame, Scorpius dragged it across the kitchen and rolled the falconer onto it. Richolf gasped in pain. "No, my lord," he said, and his master's desperation tore into Scorpius like talons.

He wrestled their dog inside to keep watch over Richolf, then ordered the cart dog to follow him to the shed, loading the fur pelts to the top for the trip back to the estate he meant to make first thing in the morning. It was late when he returned alone to the cottage, leaving the cart dog to spend the night on his own.

He returned to find Richolf had been sick over himself.

Scorpius spent a long night curled up on the pallet beside his master, offering sips of water, covering him up when he shivered, uncovering him when he sweated. Muttered words haunted the night, words that bore witness to endurance, to unyielding will. Each time Richolf woke with a start, Scorpius saw the courage marshalling behind his master's wary gaze.

Morning dawned, releasing Scorpius to set off with the pelts and return the dog and cart to their owner. Once he reached the estate, he inquired as to where he might sell the furs. When he struck out for the cottage again, it was with money and several tonics for his master.

The walk back without the dog or the estate servant gave Scorpius a chance to settle his fears and sort his thoughts. His master had never spoken directly about that night, the one that seemed to be of such dreadful importance. Now he'd been summoned to answer for the actions of that night, actions done by another, actions that swept them both up like a flash flood.

If he were to keep his grasp steady, Scorpius needed to truly understand what had gone on that day. He had it all planned, all the questions he would put to his master, until he re-entered the cottage and saw the shuttered look in Richolf's eyes.

Sitting on the edge of the pallet, Scorpius took in Richolf's pale, bruised face, mottled with dirt and sweat. How could he add himself to his master's list of tormentors?

Yet he would do it. He must succeed where the other men had failed.

20

"Sir," he said, "were they asking you about that night, when you shut me in the cupboard?"

Work-worn fingers wrapped themselves around Scorpius' hand. "No more questions," Richolf said, his voice raw with the screaming he'd done.

Scorpius closed his eyes and inhaled deeply. He must do this, even if his master begged him not to. Locking gazes with the falconer, he clasped his master's hand with both of his own. "Did you think I didn't see?"

Fear shot through Richolf's eyes. Scorpius couldn't stand to see it there.

"Dragon—"

"Yes, I know, I know," Scorpius said. "The dragon took him off, but he was already dead. Before the lord was taken out for the dragon to find, I saw what happened."

Richolf's fingers squeezed Scorpius' hand so hard he nearly yelped. His master shook his head, *no*. The falconer had been taken to the brink of what a man could stand, and he'd stuck fast to the story about the dragon. How did Scorpius think he could sway his master when burns and blows and crushing tools had not broken him?

"Sir," he said, raising his voice to speak over the falconer when he objected. "I saw the nobles fighting. I was hidden in the bushes there." He gestured toward the spot outside the cottage.

"You must swear!" Richolf said in a hoarse whisper. "The dragon is the only truth!"

"It isn't the truth!" Scorpius stood abruptly, unnerved by the shaking in his own voice. He paced across the room, glancing briefly out the window, the evening from years ago polluting the sunny afternoon. The nobles tumbling in the dust in their fine clothes, that gurgling sound the dying man had made, the way the sword had plunged into the lord so smoothly.

"The dragon must be the only thing you remember about that night," Richolf said. Scorpius turned in time to see a tear spill from the corner of his master's eye. He forgot to breathe. His master's distress cut through him, forcing him to kneel beside Richolf, his legs too weak to support him.

Yet he'd promised himself he wouldn't stop until he got the answers he needed. "Two lords fought outside the door," he said, ignoring the falconer's protests. "One of them choked the other. He was wearing a blue doublet. The third lord stabbed the fallen man to be sure he was dead. The one who died wore brown."

"You don't understand!" Richolf hissed, his voice failing him. The look of terror in his eyes swiped at Scorpius' heart like crushing talons.

"Why would they do this to you?" Scorpius asked, shaking his head at the horror that rose in his chest.

More tears fell down the falconer's scarred face, weaving through the old healed scars and the scabs of the new ones. "No one must know you were there," Richolf whispered.

"Who were they?" Scorpius said, sick at the realization that his master was close to breaking, and that it was Scorpius who had gotten farther than his master's torturers.

"Who do you think they were?" Richolf asked wearily.

"They weren't just lords. Were they?"

His master shook his head sadly. "What happened that night is only now coming to roost. The ones who fetched me to the estate are the prince's men."

"The prince," Scorpius repeated. Suddenly he wanted to stop Richolf from telling anymore.

The falconer nodded painfully. "The man who sat at this table, the one I hid you from all night in the cupboard. Lord Zorjak. Now Prince Zorjak. There will be more killing before all of this is finished."

Scorpius nodded, seeing a string of murders looming in his mind. He started when Richolf squeezed his hand once more.

"The dragon is the only thing that happened here," his master said. "Swear it."

Scorpius remembered the look of fear on his master's face when Scorpius had tumbled sleepily from the cupboard's safety that night. He remembered the polished boots of Lord Zorjak as he crawled under the table back to the cupboard. Lord Zorjak had wept that night at the news of his brother's death.

Still, Lord Zorjak's men had tortured Scorpius' master. There were still nobles who disputed the official version of Lord Nizhnii's death. Whenever unrest threatened the court, men were put to the question. The whole Nizhnii affair worked as a deterrent to any form of dissent.

"I swear, sir," Scorpius said for a second time. The first was merely to get his master inside the cottage. This time he trembled as he spoke the words. No one else would ever know that he'd seen the lords in their blue and brown velvets. It was easier to think of them as leathery scaled monstrosities.

The babies' crying filled his head, pushing him out from under the covers faster than he'd normally arise. Scorpius walked sleepily over to where Nurse and her maids dressed the little ones for their visits with their families, set to collect them today.

Once upon a time, he supposed, he'd had a little suit to receive visitors. However, the years had come and gone. No one ever came for Scorpius. Instead he helped Nurse to occupy the babies while they waited, making sure their lace collars and shiny buttons were not messed with spit-up.

A pair of elegant parents swept in and scooped up their darling, and Scorpius watched the little family leave with a horrible longing twisting in his chest. The feeling grew and grew until suddenly he was awake and lying on the pallet he'd dragged onto the kitchen floor so his master could heal upon it.

Richolf jerked and twitched on the bed, coated in sweat. Scorpius barely had time to scoot out of the way before his master bolted awake, his scream raising the hairs all over Scorpius' body.

He knew enough by now that it only made things worse if he tried to touch his master after one of these nightmares. Hanging back, he waited until Richolf's wide-eyed gaze found him as he swept the room for his torturers.

"Good morning, sir," Scorpius said in as normal a tone as he could manage.

Richolf cleared his throat. "Morning," he said gruffly.

Scorpius rose and set about feeding the dog and preparing their breakfast. His master had not been too interested in eating since returning from being questioned. How would he ever heal if he had no strength?

Kneeling beside his master, Scorpius held the plate with a plain biscuit and gave Richolf as stern a look as he dared. "You must eat, sir."

Nodding, the falconer reached for the bread and brought

it to his lips. His hand shook. The bread may as well have been made of stone, the way his teeth barely ripped a mouthful of it. Scorpius got an idea and gently took the bread back.

Tearing it into little, bite-sized pieces, he fed it to his master as though he was slipping cookies to the fussing, teething babies back at the nursery where he'd grown up. Or rewarding the falcons with bits of meat.

It took a while, but eventually the falconer managed the entire biscuit. It was the most food he'd eaten in a week. Probably longer, if Scorpius included the time his master had spent in the dungeon. His heart eased as he stood and brought the empty plate to the sideboard.

He had to leave him then to attend to the hawks out back. As he cleaned the mews and fed the birds, his mind fixated on the men who'd come here to fetch his master away to hurt him. Whenever he'd waited for the mother and father who'd never showed up for him at the nursery, he'd always assumed they would be good people, his parents. Who was to say his very father wasn't one of the men who'd made his master bleed?

As Scorpius rounded the corner of the falconer's cottage and made his way through the door, he was unprepared for the elation that filled him at the sight of his master sitting up on the pallet and stroking the dog around the ears. There was a time when he'd been certain that only the discovery of his parents' identities would ever give him such a feeling.

As he entered the cottage and Richolf's gaze softened at the sight of him, Scorpius realized he might never want to know who those two people were.

22

He should have thought it strange about the dog.

Scorpius rose from the pallet, his master's soiled bandages in his hands, just as the dog picked up its head expectantly to gaze at the door. Bleary from looking after Richolf and the falcons and the dog on his own, he didn't question the lack of barking or the slight tail wag as the door to the cottage swung open.

A woman swept inside, her strangled cry at the sight of the falconer reducing Scorpius to a stranger in his own home. She collected herself enough to ask, "Are you Scorpius?" Her stricken expression made her calm question surreal.

Looking back at his master, who lay in a half-sleep, tunic spread wide to allow for new dressings, Scorpius bowed to her and nodded.

"May I?" she asked, indicating the pallet. He nodded again and stepped aside.

She moved gracefully across the rough cottage floor, kneeling in a billow of skirt to take Richolf's face gently in both of her hands. She couldn't stop the tears then. His master's eyes opened to focus upon her face.

With surprising strength, Richolf grabbed her to him, both of them crying and kissing and laughing all at once. Scorpius had never felt the desire to be elsewhere so intensely.

Dropping the bandages in the basin, he signaled the dog to follow, slinking out into the morning. He should see to the birds, but he was so tired. He'd just take a moment.

Settling himself in the shade of a tree, he nestled in the soft grass, the dog curling beside him. When he woke the sun was past the midday position.

Getting groggily to his feet, Scorpius lurched toward the cottage, not sure at first what he'd been doing sleeping outside. As he neared the cottage door, the memory of her cry and their kisses quickened his pulse.

The dog barged past him as he paused on the threshold.

His master and the woman both sat at the table. The smell of food filled the cottage, and a dish of it sat waiting for him.

"Come," Richolf said, gesturing. "I'd like you to meet someone."

Scorpius closed the door and slid onto his chair, suddenly too shy to gaze into her face which now shone with joy.

"Scorpius, this is Ingerith."

All he could do was nod, staring instead at the feast she'd somehow conjured up while he'd slept.

"She tells me you've taken very good care of my wounds," Richolf said.

Scorpius glanced up then, to see her gazing at him with gratitude. She wasn't the most beautiful woman he'd ever seen. There had been many beauties come to the nursery to fetch their sons and daughters. Yet she was the first gently-bred woman to ever look him in the face, the first to see him. A shiver of delight ran over his skin.

23

With the arrival of Ingerith, Scorpius was free to sleep in his own bed for the first time in over a week. He hadn't realized how poorly he'd rested until that first night. No more keeping an ear out for Richolf. No more dodging out of the way before his master bolted awake from nightmares.

He awoke the morning after her arrival to find the day well underway. He leaped out of bed, hopped into his clothes and tore across the main room. He nearly collided with Ingerith, who juggled several dishes in her hands.

"Watch yourself!" Richolf barked.

He couldn't even apologize. Words lodged in his throat at the sight of his master's sweetheart once again preparing a meal for them all to share.

"Come and sit," was all she said.

Scorpius stole a glance over at Richolf, who simmered with the ill temper of a man used to full days of activity who is too long abed.

Gathering his courage, Scorpius said, "I should see to the falcons, sir. It's late."

Before his master could answer, Ingerith pulled a chair from the table and bade Scorpius to sit. "A few moments more won't be missed by the birds. You need to start your day with something in your belly. Now come."

Something about her manner made any thought except obedience completely out of the question. Scorpius walked over the stone floor and sat on the chair, gazing down at the plate of food piled generously and artfully.

Stealing a glance at his master's pallet still set up on the kitchen floor, Scorpius watched as Ingerith knelt beside his master, already coaxing a reluctant smile from his lips. Her care and her presence here had pulled Richolf from the low mood that had dogged all of Scorpius' efforts to get the falconer back on his feet.

"You mustn't give me trouble," she said to Richolf, both of

them smiling at one another. It astonished Scorpius that she could lift his master's mood so completely.

"I thought you told me it's the only thing I'm good at," Richolf said.

"It *is* the only thing you're good at," she said, forcing him to bite into a sweetcake she'd made for him.

Scorpius knew he shouldn't listen to them. He should eat up and run out back to start attending to the birds. A few of the falcons would be fussy and hard to handle by now.

Yet there was something about Ingerith that made Scorpius tingle all over whenever she spoke. Why should he hurry? She'd gone out of her way to prepare this lovely meal for him.

His master and his sweetheart laughed softly as she continued to feed him. Scorpius could not get over the shock of discovering this side of Richolf. Everything about his master brightened when she said things to him, when she smiled at him, when her fingers brushed Richolf's temple.

She worked miracles with her salves, as well. All of Richolf's burns, slashes and bruises were well on their way to disappearing since she'd come to the cottage.

Scorpius concentrated on his dish of food. He sometimes felt a stab of jealousy when all of her efforts bore such wondrous fruit, while the hours he'd stayed with Richolf, dressing the nauseating wounds and listening to the midnight ravings, had brought no relief to his master.

"... won't be able to stay much longer," she was saying.

Scorpius stopped chewing.

"I know what it means that you came out here," Richolf said.

"Yes," she said, rising to her feet. "It means you very rudely missed our appointed meeting time."

"I tried telling them that, but they'd have none of it," Richolf said.

Glancing up again, Scorpius saw the playfulness dancing in his master's eyes as he followed her movements. Was he truly joking about the torture whose memories pierced the nights with his cries?

Ingerith sat at the table beside Scorpius, leaning her chin into her palm. "When you're done eating," she said, "and when you've seen to all the birds out back, I'll need to go over his care with you."

As though she could feel the stab in his chest at the suggestion that he didn't know how to care for his master, Ingerith leaned in close. "I'll show you what all the salves and tonics are for. You'll need them. He'll be even more insufferable until he's back on his feet."

She smiled a conspiratorial grin, wrapping Scorpius in a blanket of acknowledgment that warmed him like afternoon sunlight. Still, no word would come to him. He simply nodded and forced another bite of food down his throat.

24

Standing off to the side, Scorpius tried not to watch his master's farewell to his love. Their passion filled the gray dawn, only growing in intensity the more they tried to hide it.

Finally Ingerith forced herself to step back, to turn away toward Scorpius. Her face crumpled into tears, but she walked calmly towards him as though she was fine. Glancing over at the falconer, Scorpius saw the same pained expression. Dread laced his body, his breath coming rapidly, though he did as they did and carried on as though it were a normal morning.

As Ingerith passed him and headed down the road, Scorpius locked gazes with Richolf. Warning blazed from those eyes.

No harm shall come to my beloved. No harm.

Scorpius' body went rigid with shock, never having met the side of his master that promised cool destruction. Somehow he gathered himself and nodded, man to man, before following Ingerith around the bend.

Something about the force of her strides cautioned Scorpius to keep a few paces behind her as they began their journey back to the estate. When she stopped suddenly in the road, Scorpius halted at a distance until he saw her body shudder with sobs. He was about to go to her when she turned and lunged for him.

He gasped as she grabbed him by the shoulders, her face made somehow beautiful by the ferocity of her despair. Her fingers were like talons piercing his flesh, but he refused to grimace. The unspoken order to watch over her gave him clarity now that she'd revealed herself.

"Who were they?" she said between sobs.

"Who?"

She could barely get the words out. "Who ... who hurt him?"

Now he understood. His first glimpse of Richolf huddled in the dim room at the estate had filled him with the same fury. It had given him the words to make the guard jump to his demands.

It was hard to look into her eyes. The pain behind them shook Scorpius harder than her crushing hands. Yet he forced himself to do it anyway. "My lady," he began, then grunted out as she shoved him to the ground.

"I am not a lady. Don't call me that!"

Scorpius scrambled to his knees, keeping her in his sights. He raised both hands before him in a halting gesture. "My apologies, Ingerith."

"Who hurt him?" She stood over him, and every instinct cautioned him to retreat, but he held his ground. The look on his master's face as they'd departed made more sense now. The danger Richolf had faced had not ended in the dungeon.

Well, Scorpius would not betray him. The horror of the wounds Richolf still wore deserved to be honored. "I don't know their names, lady — Ingerith."

She grabbed his tunic and shook him. Scorpius held onto her hands and braced himself against her onslaught. "Don't start!" she said. "Tell me what they looked like. What were they wearing?"

It would be so easy to describe them. He would remember everything about that afternoon as long as he lived. "I don't know — they were just nobles come for a hunt."

Ingerith froze, her expression rapidly reevaluating Scorpius. She released him and strode away for a few moments. He got to his feet, wary of her next move, haunted by his master's gaze as they'd left.

"Don't you want to help him?" she said finally. She turned and looked at Scorpius, and he no longer felt like a boy looking at a woman. She looked so fragile. He felt like he should comfort her. And he recognized this as the greatest threat of all.

"He never broke," he said, gesturing back towards the cottage. "Whatever it was they wanted from him, he never gave it to them. I will do as he commands me. That is how I can help him."

She closed the distance between them. "I know people," she said, just as cool as Richolf's warning. "They can make those bastards suffer."

Scorpius shook his head, *no*.

Ingerith took a deep breath. "I will make inquiries. It will merely speed things if you tell me now."

Bowing his head, Scorpius remained silent. When she did nothing but stare at him, he moved forward along the road in the direction of the estate. "Come!" he said at last when she gazed back toward her love who remained hidden beyond the curve of the road.

Ingerith wiped her tears from her face, turned back to face the road and began walking. Yet it was merely the ghostly remains of the woman who'd brought smiles to his master's battered face.

For a terrible moment Scorpius almost told her. Why shouldn't they suffer, if she knew someone who could make that happen?

Instead, he set the pace for the long walk back to the estate. He ignored her crying which didn't stop for a long, long time. When they reached a certain landmark known only to her, she told him to stay.

"No one must see me with the falconer's boy," she said.

He nodded, watching her wipe her face with a delicate pocket cloth. She smoothed her hair and brushed the dust from her skirts. Then she turned and walked to his side, placing a kiss on the top of his head.

"I know you'll keep him safe. Remember all the things I told you about the salves."

"Yes, miss."

Then she walked down the lane and out of sight.

Scorpius decided the safest thing to do would be to duck into the woods beside the road itself for a time. He followed the route from a discreet distance, pausing like those little game hens behind the safety of the branches every time a traveler appeared in the road.

When he finally spied the falconer's cottage, he stood in the dappled shade and took in the sight of the falconer standing watch at the door. He eventually emerged to rejoin his master and settle him back on the pallet.

He didn't shrink from the penetrating stare, heavy with questions. No more was said of Ingerith for some time, as though she'd never arrived with her smiles, her tonics or her tears.

25

The urge to gouge his eyes out spun him away from the scene but it was too late. He'd seen them.

Scorpius crashed through the brush like wounded prey. He should flee as silently as he'd stumbled upon the two of them, but the need to put distance between himself and detection cautioned speed.

Branches whipped his face. Unseen dips in the forest floor grabbed to take him down. Scorpius ran on. They must never suspect he was anything but a startled animal.

They.

His master's love, Ingerith, entwined in the arms of a man who was not Richolf. Far worse — the man was a noble, his steed grazing quietly a few yards off.

He cursed the gods for leading him to that particular spot in the forest. For giving him the afternoon away from his duties, for Richolf's leave granted to enjoy the day in any way he saw fit.

How could he enjoy anything anymore? She was untrue. It was only a matter of time before Richolf's heart — the heart that was braver than any man's — would suffer the killing stroke at last.

Scorpius kept running until his chest burned for air. He stopped by a brook which meandered over stones and under moss, sitting himself upon a flat rock that cooled him. Scooping water to his lips, he drank and then splashed a few handfuls over his face.

He looked back the way he had come. Nothing stirred. Nothing made a sound.

He didn't think they'd seen him. How could they, when they were so intent on devouring one another's mouths?

If only he could doubt that it had really been Ingerith. Yet the gods offered no kindnesses for the likes of him. She'd gazed straight in his direction when he'd first come upon them, creeping forward unseen behind the leaves and shadows. She'd gazed but hadn't seen him, her attention quickly turning back to the noble who ran his hands along her body with possessive familiarity.

How would he be able to keep such a thing from his master?

Scorpius' stomach clenched at the prospect. All he could think of was the way she'd coaxed those smiles from Richolf when his body lay broken after the questioning, several years past. For that, Scorpius would always be grateful to her. For that alone, he would have kept her terrible deceit to himself.

Yet he was only an apprentice who served the falconer. What business did he have, an unclaimed boy given over to a master, to open his mouth only to cause fighting or even bloodshed? Such knowledge could lead to very dark places.

If he were honest with himself, withholding the information from Richolf was really a little seed of hope. The ways of men and women were foreign to Scorpius, who'd spent half his life now in the company of his master and the men who came to the hunt. Perhaps there was something he just didn't understand.

The little seed was soon pulverized when he arrived at the falconer's cottage to see the same steed from the forest tied to a post in the yard.

His master and the noble turned at the same time to regard Scorpius as he rounded the corner of the mews and found them just as Richolf secured a falcon to his gloved forearm. Scorpius' body froze, his heart beating like the furious flight of a doomed game bird. It was the same noble. The same.

It was the man who'd strode down to the rushes with Scorpius, who'd peppered him with questions, who'd taken the game-flushing stick to leave a burning welt along the back of Scorpius' head. The noble who'd crushed Ingerith's body to his own, just now in the forest, it was the same man.

Scorpius barely had time to lower his gaze before the noble could return it. Just enough time to see the blank expression on his master's suddenly gray face.

The memory of Richolf's wounds rose up to shake Scorpius

violently inside. He looked at the noble's hand and remembered how it had swung the stick to strike him, how it had just run along Ingerith's body in the forest.

"I wasn't expecting you," Richolf said, his voice betraying nothing.

Quick — he must think of something. Anything. "I got hungry, sir. Saw the mount and hurried down, sir."

Richolf nodded to the noble, who led the way out of the mews. "As there is only this one lord for the hunt, you may eat," his master said.

Scorpius nodded and struck out for the cottage, watching the lord stride across the field with his master. His palms grew sticky with sweat. He must follow them. He must keep his master safe. No one would ever hurt his master like that again.

Wrapping his fingers around the knife he always kept strapped to his hip, Scorpius slipped between trunks and around rock ledges, keeping the two men in sight. The feel of the knife handle lessened his trembling. He knew how accidents could happen to the wrong noble on the wrong hunt.

26

Richolf had barely released the falcon when the noble grabbed him by the hair and forced him writhing to his knees. "What game are you playing?" the lord asked, a note of amusement in his voice.

Scorpius rose from his half-crouch, concealed by the forest. The knife slipped from its sheath like his next breath. Yet he must wait. He must wait.

"No games, my lord." Richolf twisted in pain but made no sound.

"Do you know, I've just now left my newest diversion? Met her for a tumble in the woods a ways back there." The noble tightened his hold on Richolf's hair and shook the falconer. His master's eyes screwed shut. "You see, the odd thing was, we had no plan to meet up this morning. I just came across her on the road. Don't you find that strange?"

"Yes, my lord," Richolf gasped. "Very strange." His face lined with dismay. The words upset him more than even the noble's grip upon him, it seemed.

With sudden viciousness, the lord kicked Richolf to the ground. With his polished boot he crushed the falconer's face into the dust. Scorpius' fingers gripped his knife handle as he readied himself, remaining hidden as though chained there.

"I never suspected you'd been running a little love nest out here, falconer," the noble said. "Very shrewd."

"No, my lord. I haven't."

"No?" He stomped harder on Richolf's head. His master cried out then. "Then what would a governess be doing out here, all alone? Hmm?"

When Richolf didn't answer, the noble grabbed him up to his knees again, grabbing fistfuls of doublet. For a long moment he gazed deeply into Richolf's eyes, finally smiling a terrible smile. "We both know you can keep a secret. Don't we?"

Scorpius' heart chilled as his master bowed his head and said nothing.

"You held out for days when we wanted to know what happened to Nizhnii. Dragon, was it?" He shoved Richolf and took several strides away from him.

The falconer collected himself but stayed on his knees, bracing for anything. Scorpius knew his master had his own knife strapped to his hip. Why didn't he reach for it?

The noble stopped and gazed into the forest for a long moment. When he finally turned back to face Richolf, his expression promised bloodshed. Scorpius crept forward, as close as he dared without giving himself away.

"I'm not one to stop a man from making a few coins when he can," the lord said. "I salute your enterprise, falconer. Who better to ensure that our indiscretions remain hidden from wagging tongues?"

He strode towards Richolf, who did not shrink or falter, only lowered his gaze as he must. "Other tongues will spill, though, won't they?"

The noble turned and walked away from the hunt he'd never been interested in. Richolf remained on his knees until the lord was out of sight.

As his master got to his feet, running a shaking hand through his hair and gazing after the noble with a look of pure fear, Scorpius nearly stepped out of the shelter of leaves and branches. Yet something cautioned him, something held him back.

He waited until Richolf went to collect the falcon from where it pecked hungrily at the game it had brought down. Gazing down at the knife still gripped tightly in his hand, Scorpius wondered what it would have felt like to plunge the blade into the noble's belly.

27

Scorpius ran as though demons and dragons were on his heels. When Richolf returned to the cottage, he must never suspect Scorpius had witnessed this latest insult from the noble.

He wove and dodged through the brush, silent and swift. Why hadn't his master slipped out his own knife? Perhaps if Scorpius had made his presence known, maybe if his master had realized there were two against one, perhaps the noble would have been made to pay for his master's treatment.

All he had to do was recall the expressions of dread upon the guards' faces that night, when the prince had arrived to collect his brother. In truth, it was Richolf and himself who were surrounded. There would be no satisfaction for insults suffered at the hands of any noble who chose to remind a falconer as to who served whom.

For a winded moment he stood before the door, wondering if there was any chance his master could have reached it before him. Upon entering the cottage, he found it empty. His ragged breathing filled their home.

Scorpius wearily scrounged a few bites of food as he'd been told to do, guiltily chewing as he remembered the look of pain on his master's face. Richolf had known it was bound to happen, hadn't he? That's why he'd sent Scorpius away instead of welcoming the assistance of his apprentice on the hunt.

There were things a master did not want his apprentice to see. Scorpius had not listened, and so he was now a witness to things he would never be able to strike from his memory. He stopped chewing, the biscuit dry in his mouth.

From now on, he would obey. From now on, he would be an apprentice his master could be proud of.

It was hard not to jump in alarm when Richolf finally flew through the door. However, Scorpius could not let on he expected anything other than a slightly tired master back from serving at the hunt.

Luckily, the look of panic on the falconer's face would have been enough to make him drop his food in the dish, which is what he did. Scorpius got to his feet. "Sir, what's the—"

"I need you to hurry to the estate." Richolf dashed into his room for ink and paper.

Scurrying to set his dish on the sideboard, grabbing up his leather satchel, Scorpius longed to ask his master what was going on. He'd just now resolved to be good, hadn't he? Could he not keep that promise for even a moment?

He stood ready and waiting, listening to the *scratch-scratch* of writing. Richolf rounded the corner into the main room, his attention very far away. He'd neglected to wipe the dirt from his face. Scorpius looked down, reminding himself he would have remarked upon it if he hadn't already witnessed its origin.

Handing the sealed paper to him, Richolf said, "This must get to Ingerith."

Scorpius looked up, making sure he stared pointedly at the dirt still clinging to his master's temple and beard. "Yes, sir."

Richolf rubbed at the dirt, irritated. When recognition dawned, the defenseless expression clouding his master's face made Scorpius want to turn away. He swallowed hard.

The falconer drew himself up, as if shrugging off the fear that still darted through his eyes. He ushered Scorpius through the door. "You must not give this directly to her, you understand."

"No, sir."

Taking one of Scorpius' hands in his, he pressed several coins into his palm. "You may need these."

Scorpius gazed down at the money, the danger pressing down on him. So many questions. Yet he would ask none of them.

Nodding once, he set off at a jog away from the cottage, not looking back. He'd had his fill of seeing that which his master did not want him to see.

28

Twisted log to the left, a ways back. He was on the right path. Jogging to stay ahead of his jittery nerves, Scorpius kept his sights forward, looking for the second marker.

This one was harder to see. Luckily, he was used to finding game birds sitting silently in their camouflage. A mossy stump, blending seamlessly with cool leaves, barely caught his eye. Scorpius halted, listening carefully, scanning the forest to be certain he wasn't being followed.

He turned to face south. To one of the residents of the estate, it might seem that there was no path in that direction at all. Yet to a hunter, the way beckoned, clear and insistent.

Making his way over and under, pressing through the dense weave of branches, Scorpius neared the meeting place. Something his master had expressly forbidden.

You must not give this directly to her, you understand.

Scorpius stepped out of the trees into a gorge that opened up without warning. Two rock faces blocked the sun, making him shiver in the cooler air. The cliffs were heavily overgrown with moss, bracken and decaying logs. No paths found their way down. There were no signs of any human travel through the ravine.

The evidence of isolation brought comfort. This was the place.

Choosing a tucked-away lookout, Scorpius settled upon a long-ago toppled tree to await his master's unfaithful lover. He wasn't sure why the memory of another man's hands upon her should hurt so much. Nor why his cheeks flushed.

He tried to think of something else as he waited, but his mind was full of her. He thought of the smile which had filled their cottage with joy. He remembered the sound of her throaty laugh, which had lifted his heart even as it stirred his body.

Fidgeting on his perch, Scorpius stilled when he thought he heard something. There it was again.

Ingerith emerged into the ravine clad in tones of brown and

black, the need for discretion demanding her face be concealed by a wrap. Scorpius rose to greet her, when a terrible notion struck him. What if this wasn't Ingerith?

He froze, his heart thudding loudly, so loudly he was certain she could hear it. What if she revealed herself and it was a complete stranger? Could she be trusted to bring Ingerith a message?

Perhaps this woman was here only to tie up some irritating loose ends for the royal brother in brown brocade.

Scorpius shut his eyes, remembering the terrible wounds his master once wore. The look of absolute dread on Richolf's face when Scorpius had tumbled out of the cabinet, so near to discovery by the murderous prince. The sound made by the brother as the sword was drawn from his chest.

His master knew intimately the consequences of failure. Yet knowing all of this, he'd still sent his apprentice to bring a message to Ingerith. Richolf must have some sort of faith in him.

Scooping up his courage from where it had tumbled away into the ravine, Scorpius drew a deep breath and opened his eyes, just as the woman drew the kerchief down to reveal her face.

29

Ingerith gazed at him, haughty and frightened. Her lips parted as she caught her breath, her cheeks flushing so prettily. A cautious gaze in every direction made her seem like a girl scrambling to avoid self-made trouble. When she closed the distance between herself and Scorpius, she moved like a queen.

He returned her gaze as long as he dared. When finally he bowed his head, Scorpius' skin tingled with her nearness.

"You were not followed?" she asked, a note of admiration in her voice if he wasn't mistaken.

"No, miss."

Reaching down to lift her skirts, Ingerith ran her fingers along her stocking, along her thigh to a garter that hugged her there. Scorpius was certain he should not be witness to this. Yet there was no one here but the two of them. Besides, he'd already seen her with her skirts a-tumble in the woods that day. Though she didn't know that.

He watched as she slipped a sealed note from between the garter and her firm skin. Swallowing against the lump that seemed to block his throat, Scorpius held a hand out to accept the message from her. When she kept it back from him, he looked up into her eyes.

They danced with amusement and… something else.

"This is for your master's eyes only."

Scorpius' face grew hot with annoyance. "Of course," he snapped.

Lifting her chin and an eyebrow, Ingerith offered the message to him a second time. Scorpius reached out and took it, being very careful not to make contact with her. He wasn't sure why.

"In the event that something happens to it," she said, gesturing regally at the note, "I need you to remember three words."

Scorpius was about to protest that he wouldn't let anything happen to the message when his master's lover placed two fingers over his lips. He couldn't prevent a gasp escaping him.

Her eyes met his, welling with raw emotion. His heart forgot to beat as she loosened the ribbons at her neck, tugging her neckline to the side, exposing her throat. An ugly red welt encircled her there.

At first he couldn't imagine how such a mark could have got there. Then he remembered which man Ingerith had laid with in the woods that day. He remembered the blow which that same noble had given him, and the horrible burns and bruises and torn flesh his master had returned with, from that noble's questioning.

Ingerith retied the ribbons, bowing her own head under his scrutiny. When she finally looked up again, her face was clouded with shame. How it hurt him to see it. He'd dreamt of seeing it, had burned to see it in the private moments of the night.

Now he would give anything if she would only cloak herself in her imperious manner. Anything so he wouldn't have to admit to himself that nothing was as black and white as he wanted it to be.

Taking a deep breath, Ingerith said, "Promise you'll remember."

"I swear it," he said, recalling how his own master had spoken those words after kneeling before the lord who had murdered in the name of the prince. Bending his knee, Scorpius lowered himself before Ingerith. It was a relief to be forced to look up at her.

Her face took on a resolute gravity. Not the arrogance he'd craved, but it would do. She took hold of his shoulders. "The words are 'talon', 'gauntlet' and 'jess.'"

"'Talon', 'gauntlet' and 'jess,'" he repeated.

Her fingers grabbed him by the chin and forced him to look into her face. Ingerith's eyes now blazed with warning, and that was so much better than the suffering that had darkened her face, moments before. It felt good that her grip was too tight. It served him right for having wished something like the mark around her neck upon her.

"Again," she said.

He said it as many times as she demanded it. She released him without warning, striding away to head back into the forest. "Remain here for awhile. We cannot be seen together," she cautioned.

"Yes, miss," he said as she gave him one final glance. Then she wrapped her kerchief over her face and slipped between the trees into the shadows.

30

He barely noticed the darkening of the sky through the dense canopy of trees, until the persistent *drip-drip* began to fall on his lashes. Blinking away the vision of Ingerith, of her haughty stare and her smooth curves beckoning from the drape of her bodice, Scorpius tapped the message she'd given to him and tucked securely beneath his vest.

Satisfied that it was still there, he increased his pace, glancing up at the heavy sky. Just when he would have appreciated the protection of the forest, his path took him onto the road now bordered by scrub brush and boulders. Before long he was splashing through puddles, the rain coming in sheets.

He finally rushed up to the door of their cottage, shaking the water from his fingertips before going inside.

His master greeted him wordlessly, tossing him a linen to wrap around himself. As Scorpius shrugged out of his vest, he grabbed it back from where he'd been about to drop it on the sodden pile. Fishing around for the pocket opening, his heart stilled as he realized the message was soft and about to fall apart at his touch.

He looked up in alarm at Richolf.

His master returned his gaze with a dawning understanding. Turning, he strode across the room, rubbing a hand over his face.

Scorpius carefully retrieved the soaked message, as limp as pastry dough. He laid it on the corner of the table, wishing the cottage was somehow bigger. He peeled out of his leggings and grabbed the linen tightly to cover himself, standing awkwardly for a long moment as Richolf said nothing.

His master had never been one to raise his voice. Still, Scorpius could feel the unspoken shouting hanging in the air between them. Collecting the drenched bundle of clothes in one arm, he dumped them into a bucket, turning to see his master sit at the table.

Richolf stared unseeing at the wooden surface. More than

anything, Scorpius wished he could dash past his master and burrow under his blankets. However, the falconer had not raised him to be such a coward. Forcing his feet to take him forward, Scorpius took his own seat at the table.

"I don't suppose you read it," Richolf said, finally.

"No, sir." He wanted to look up, to look into his master's eyes. He wanted Richolf to know how sorry he was, while he dreaded the disappointment he knew would meet him.

The memory of Ingerith's gaze blazing down at him in the forest jogged him to recall the words she'd bade him repeat. "Talon," he blurted without warning. "Gauntlet. Jess."

Richolf rose and stood there for a terrible moment. He walked slowly to stand beside Scorpius. "What did you say?" he whispered.

"Talon," Scorpius said as clearly as he could, though he shook. "Gauntlet. Jess."

"In that order?" Richolf said, his voice stronger now.

"Yes, sir."

His master walked to the door and strode out into the downpour. Scorpius didn't see him again for two days.

31

Returning from the mews, Scorpius rounded the corner of the cottage to discover a dozen mounts and several guards lounging on the grass beside them. Before he could panic, several nobles filed out of the cottage door, laughing and talking, followed by Richolf. The guards rose to their feet.

His master moved to the side as several noblewomen swept through the door and into the sunlight. Scorpius had never heard of women being on any hunt. His body chilled in alarm.

His master caught sight of him and called him over with a nearly imperceptible jerk of his head. Obeying Richolf at a run, he skirted the line of nobles and ladies and was at his master's side in a trice.

Richolf began to list supplies he required in a low voice meant for Scorpius alone. Interrupting his master, though his gut warned him not to do it, Scorpius said, "I've fed them all." He flicked his head toward the mews and their falcons. "I didn't know they were coming."

A satisfied hawk made for a poor hunt.

Richolf's eyes shadowed with haunted disbelief. One of the nobles noticed their exchange and joined them.

"Problem, falconer?" he said, his voice measured but his gaze hard.

For one moment Richolf hesitated. Then he grabbed a fistful of Scorpius' tunic, yanked him close and slapped him twice across the face.

Scorpius gasped in shock. The cruel set to his master's face turned Richolf into a sudden stranger, his mouth a grim line as he shook Scorpius to rattle his brains.

"Ready the red-tail, the gray and the king hawk," Richolf said, shoving Scorpius away so that he nearly sprawled on the ground before the nobles and guards.

Face burning from the blows and disgrace, Scorpius took off for the mews as fast as his legs would carry him. Why hadn't he waited an hour longer to feed the bloody birds? There had been any number of jobs to do before getting to the falcons. He and his master had put together hunting parties more than once for nobles that showed up at any time without warning.

A hungry hawk was a precision hunter. A hungry hawk ensured a successful hunt. A successful hunt sent away happy nobles.

Bursting into the red-tailed mews, Scorpius set the falcon flapping as he rushed through his preparations. Of all the hunts to set out from a bad footing, his master didn't need the ladies to witness a poor showing on their first time in the field.

Slamming the supplies into a leather satchel, Scorpius grabbed up the jesses and fought to settle the bird on his arm. He scurried to join the party as it ambled in high-spirited conversation along the corridor created by the mews.

Richolf waited grimly beside the noble. Rejoining his master, Scorpius extended his arm so Richolf could transfer the falcon to the noble's gauntlet-clad arm.

Dashing away before he could meet his master's gaze, Scorpius learned nothing from his encounter with the red-tail, sending the gray into flustered screeching with his sloppy grabbing and yanking. By the time he'd delivered the king hawk to his master, Scorpius knew the strange master who had returned from those two days he'd been gone without a word would have something to say about his apprentice, once the hunt was over.

32

Scorpius stood in the shadows at the forest's edge. His poor judgment in feeding the falcons, not realizing that a hunt was imminent, had not resulted in catastrophe after all. He watched the dependable red-tail take down the game hen he'd just flushed from the bushes. A smattering of applause from the ladies' gloved hands traveled on the breeze.

He caught sight of one of the guards a short distance away, ever vigilant. Still smarting from Richolf's blows, Scorpius turned away from the imposing young man, the sort of fellow who would never disappoint his master. Ever.

Scorpius' heart sank when he heard the guard approach after several moments. He was in no mood to make conversation with a golden boy. Especially one who had witnessed him receiving his first physical correction at his master's hands.

The guard swaggered over with an appraising air, nodding once in greeting. They stood in blessed silence for a time, gazing out at the hunt, watching as the dog trotted back to Richolf with the game hen.

Dipping his hand into a pocket inside his leather jerkin, the guard retrieved a flat biscuit, snapping it in half. He offered a piece to Scorpius, who accepted the food though he was anything but hungry.

Up close, it easy to see the faint slash scars peppering the guard's jaw and temple, forearms and hands. Weapons practice, likely. Scorpius once sported scars from the falcons when he was younger, learning how to handle the birds. The guard's scars somehow carried more prestige than his own faded marks from the king hawk's talons.

"It's a good place out here," the young man said.

Scorpius shrugged. "Serves us well."

"You'd think Lord Dirske would have staged one of his entertainments out here before this."

They'd certainly never had this many nobles at one hunt before, and never had there been any noblewomen out here.

Did that make it an entertainment? "Far as I know," Scorpius said, "all of our guests have had good results here. My master ensures a successful hunt." His skin prickled at how close he'd come to casting a blot on Richolf's reputation.

The guard looked at him sideways, a wicked grin playing over his lips. "Well, aren't you the sly pup."

Scorpius felt certain the guard misunderstood him. Yet the young man was so delighted, all of a sudden. Gazing back out at the hunt, Scorpius waited for a signal from Richolf.

When it came, he dashed to the next course point that held the highest likelihood of sheltering game. He didn't think again about the young guard's words until much later, closer to sunset, after he and Richolf had roasted the game for the nobles. A small retinue of servants brought along for the event laid out a vast feast to which the fresh meat was the centerpiece.

Marveling at the amount of food, at the raucous level of celebration, Scorpius wondered if it was always like this with the nobles. Neither the guards, nor the servants, nor his master seemed to bat an eye at the noise and at the way they carried on.

As the day lengthened into evening, the arrival of yet another group caught Scorpius' attention. He straightened, wondering how they would accommodate so many new guests. Looking to Richolf for direction, he watched his master take one look at them and turn away, his face a grimace, his head shaking.

Scorpius didn't understand until he heard the crying.

When he looked closer, he realized this new group was made up of slaves, bound to one another and huddled in the grass near the corner of the closest mews. The young guard he'd encountered earlier was in charge of them. He bent his head low to speak to the girl in tears.

The other guards shifted their weight uneasily, one whispering heatedly, "Will you shut her up?"

Lord Dirske stood staring at them all from across the field. By the expressions on the guards' faces, something had not gone according to plan.

Richolf joined Scorpius as the crying slave girl finally ruffled the attention of the entire hunting party. "Gods save us," his master said, as though certain they'd already abandoned every one of them.

33

The young slave raced away from the others, driven onto the open field by a shove and the crack of a whip. Her body gleamed in the torchlight, the sound of her ragged breathing tearing the air and battering Scorpius' chest. She got about as far as a game hen would have reached.

To the approving roar of the assembled nobles, one of the lords tore after her, his battle-hardened body closing the distance between himself and his prey in seconds. Stripped down to leggings and boots, unencumbered by sword or finery, the noble cut an impressive figure as he tackled the slave to the ground, rolling them both to a stop.

Scorpius' heart seized with dread, just as it had done the Night of the Cupboard, just as it had done when he'd entered the sick room to collect Richolf. Protesting incoherently as the crowd applauded the capture, the slave pushed at her attacker but he would not be denied.

His master steadied Scorpius by the shoulders when he tried to recoil. "Don't look away," Richolf said in the barest of whispers. "There are eyes everywhere. Our enthusiasm as hosts must not be questioned."

Nodding once, his heart sickened by the display, Scorpius glanced over at the group of frightened slaves and wondered why only one of them had cried before it all began.

The chase was repeated until every slave had been run down and plundered by a noble. Scorpius hoped that none of those eyes keeping watch had seen his tears when the crying slave was forced onto the field.

At first he didn't see Lord Dirske, but all at once he caught a glimpse of the noble shrugging back into his doublet, emerging from the darkness. Scorpius started backwards, but Richolf's solid form prevented him from retreating. Grateful for the night with its cloak of shadows, Scorpius worked hard to pull himself together, hoping his tears had dried on his face.

"I have a bit of business with my guard detail," the noble

said. "Where do you take care of that sort of thing?"

Richolf paused, but only for a moment. "The... ah... the hitching posts, out front."

"A bit of a trek, that. Nothing to hand?"

"I must consider the falcons, my lord. They're likely to join in the screeching. Can be rather ear-splitting."

"Ah. Well, the hitching post it is, then."

The gold-haired guard who'd shared his food with Scorpius made his measured way along the corridor between the mews, hemmed in by four of his fellows. Scorpius followed behind Richolf, who followed behind Lord Dirske. They rounded the cottage, which was being readied to house the most regal of the guests for the night.

Scorpius glanced with longing at the warm glow of the windows, knowing he was barred from his own bed. If only this was a nightmare.

There was no waking from the sight of the young guard removing his jerkin and tunic. *Why was this happening? What had the guard done, exactly?*

Sick with dread, Scorpius watched as the young man was pushed to his knees, his wrists tied to one of the wooden posts. Uncoiling his lash from his belt, the sergeant stepped forward and silently offered the guard a folded piece of leather to bite upon.

The young man took the leather in his teeth and looked up for a moment at his commander. Something passed between them, something that helped the guard to brace himself.

The sergeant had barely turned to take up his stance behind the guard when Lord Dirske strode up to yank the leather from the young man's mouth. "It was *their* sniveling I didn't want to hear," he said. "I'm very much interested in yours."

34

L ord Dirske rejoined Richolf and Scorpius, leaning in to say, "So far I've been pleased with this event, Falconer. This is merely housekeeping."

Richolf nodded but said nothing, glancing down at Scorpius, his eyes shadowed with warning. Scorpius' heart pounded in his chest. He didn't want this to happen. He didn't want to be here. Yet the noble stood right beside them. There was nowhere for Scorpius to go.

Lord Dirske got what he requested at the very first cut of the lash. The young guard, who'd seemed so worldly and seasoned when they'd stood together watching the hunt, now screamed so that Scorpius' hair stood on end. He couldn't look, repelled by the way the young guard's body flailed against his bonds. There was no way to stop up Scorpius' ears.

He was a heartbeat away from puking by the time the young guard was cut out of his bonds. How he wished he hadn't glanced up at that very moment when two men from the detachment took the faltering guard by the arms and dragged him away. It was only a glance, but it was enough. More than enough.

Lord Dirske turned to Richolf, making final adjustments to his doublet. "The cottage will make for a nice little nest," he said, a terrible smile playing over his face.

Richolf simply bowed smartly and deeply. "My pleasure to serve, my lord."

The noble turned while Richolf was still in the midst of speaking and strode away. Scorpius' master froze for a moment. Then he let out a deep sigh, straightened and ran a hand through his hair.

"I want you to find out where they took that poor bastard," Richolf said in a low voice. "Get him some water, some fresh cloths to clean him up with. You can't enter the cottage. You'll have to take the bandages from the hawk supplies."

"Yes, sir," Scorpius said. He dashed off in the direction

they'd dragged the young fellow. It didn't take long to spot the huddle of guards and to hear the moans of the one who'd failed to silence the only slave to have responded to her circumstances as logically as possible.

Scorpius passed the supplies to the man who'd swung the lash. Up close, he could see the dismay in the older man's eyes at what had just transpired. The young guard's moans continued in a stream of mindless suffering. Glad to be rid of his duty, Scorpius hurried away to rejoin Richolf, but his master was not where he'd left him.

Once he found him, Richolf ordered Scorpius to do this for the nobles and that for the servants, ensuring that everyone had whatever it was they needed.

Scorpius resorted to shaking his head and hopping in place to stay awake so he could assist his master. Once everyone was settled, Richolf chose a patch beneath a giant tree and stretched himself out. With a private nod between just them, Richolf motioned for Scorpius to join him.

Lying on the lumpy grass beside his master, he returned Richolf's sad gaze for a long moment. Then the falconer reached out his hand and brushed Scorpius' cheek where it was still tender from the blows his master had given him at the start of this nightmare hunt.

How mortified Scorpius had felt to suffer that first physical correction before this assembly.

Problem, falconer? Lord Dirske had asked, just after Scorpius had informed Richolf of his error in judgment, the one that had led him to feed the hawks before the hunt. His master had hesitated. Panic had flooded his master's eyes, panic stemming from Richolf knowing only too well what type of man was asking as to whether Scorpius had created a problem.

Before Richolf's hand withdrew from Scorpius' cheek, Scorpius reached up and clasped it with his own. A bruise was not a lacerated back. Hurt feelings and confusion when he hadn't realized, well they were not the same as those shrieks the guard had made.

35

His master didn't have to light a fire under Scorpius when it came to removing any sign that the hunt of screams had contaminated their cottage. Richolf and Scorpius collected and burned the refuse, removed and soaked the bedding, swept and scrubbed every surface the nobles had touched.

Distress still rattled around inside of Scorpius, but the hectic pace of the work kept him one step ahead of remembering. Still, the sounds of the hunt repeated themselves in his mind. It was the sounds that he couldn't escape. Sleeplessness warped his vision so that he dropped things, missed what he reached for and had to make three trips when one would have sufficed.

Taking a short break, Richolf found one nearly-empty tankard and poured a mug of ale for himself. He just reached out to grab it when Scorpius stepped into a patch of soapy water.

His feet shot out from under him. Flinging his arms out to stop his fall, Scorpius knocked the mop handle which had leaned against the table. The mug of ale flew into Richolf's chest. The last of the brew soaked his master's tunic, the mug rattling and bouncing off the wall, the mop clattering to the floor. Scorpius knocked his head against the flagstones and fought for breath as the wind knocked out of him.

He rolled and gasped like a fish, lungs seizing painfully. Then his gut relaxed and breath inflated his body once again. He sprawled on the floor until he realized his master was laughing.

Scorpius rose to his knees. Richolf hunched over the table, slapping it as though he couldn't get the laughs out fast enough.

For a moment, Scorpius knelt there, soaked and sore, still getting his breath back. His master's hair dripped with the ale he hadn't had the pleasure of drinking. The dog stood at the ready, tail half-wagging with the uproar coming from the falconer.

He couldn't listen to the laughter without joining in. It was too contagious. When he took a moment to think about it, the way he must have looked as he tried to break his fall, at the look on his master's face as the mug was struck from his grasp, well it just made him laugh harder.

When the dog sniffed around and discovered the dashed contents of the mug, licking it up with relish, Scorpius and his master howled until they cried.

When they'd had their fill of it, Richolf bundled up an extra set of clothes for both of them and bade Scorpius to join him at the stream. They walked together in silence, the sun warm and renewing as though nothing terrible could have happened only hours earlier.

Reaching the deep bend in the stream where they bathed, the two of them peeled their wet garments off, reeking of soap and ale. They waded into the water, beginning seriously enough but soon degenerating into horseplay. Water splashed everywhere. Richolf dunked Scorpius, while Scorpius nearly dunked the falconer but not quite.

When they tired of even that, they crawled onto the bank and stretched out on the grass to dry off. At that moment, it didn't matter to Scorpius that his master sported such gruesome scars that he could never quite escape seeing. It didn't matter that a lump had formed on the back of his head from the fall, which now throbbed.

For a moment, he felt clean and warm and spent from laughing. He would hold onto this moment so that he could find it again in the dark hours of the night.

36

He watched the sweep of Ingerith's skirt as she disappeared around the crest of the boulder.

Scorpius scanned the sky for dragon signs, but in truth he sought to avoid hearing the bittersweet laughter, the muffled sounds of his master and his master's lover.

An hour passed while Scorpius sat on watch.

In passing the warning to Richolf that the Nightmare Hunt was bound for their cottage, Ingerith's safety was too much at risk for more trysts. Her current noble patron had proven himself to be a cruel benefactor.

So Scorpius scanned the horizon, doing his best to keep his mind on snaps of twigs in the brush instead of latching onto the way Richolf cradled his lover behind their screen of granite. Insistent moans brought horrible images to mind from the slave hunt several nights' past, and Scorpius fought the urge to rise and pace the memories away.

Dwarfing leathery wingspan or vindictive lord — which was worse? The shrieks of his little nursery friend just before the dragon fire burnt her down to cinders that morning, or the cries of the slave as Lord Dirske pierced her body before the cheering assembly — their pleading haunted him the moment he sat in stillness.

Hugging his knees to his chest, Scorpius thought about the guard who'd shared his food with him before the hunt had turned gruesome. He must have known what the evening would bring. He'd even grinned at him and said, *Well, aren't you the sly pup*, when Scorpius had assured him his master provided successful hunts.

A strong sense of outrage goaded Scorpius. He wanted to feel repulsed by that young man, yet how could he find fault when the guard's attempt to stop the crying slave from disrupting the hunt's surprise had not been blows but quiet words? If he were truthful with himself, he'd admired the way in which the guard had walked toward his penance with calm dignity.

Yet it made Scorpius' skin crawl with shame to admit it, when clearly the guard had known what was about to unfold, even as he'd offered to share that food.

Ingerith wept softly now. Couldn't this dreadful afternoon come to an end?

Scorpius shifted his seat on the boulder, unable to find a spot that didn't dig into his flesh. He wished that his master had not required a lookout this afternoon. Yet, if a noble such as Lord Dirske had taken him to serve on his estate, would he have been able to bear each day as the young guard did?

What would his life have amounted to, if it had been someone like Lord Dirske to collect him? Not as an apprentice, not as a servant, but as kin. If his father had been such a man, what would Scorpius himself be like now?

Tears welled in his eyes. For a moment he resisted them.

The sounds that came from behind the boulder should have belonged to his master and Ingerith alone. Scorpius let the hot sorrow roll down his face with no one to see or hear.

37

SCORPIUS, AGED 16 YEARS

Scorpius watched as his master struggled to tie up the pelts for delivery to the estate. The dampness of the past three days of rain had taken its toll on the falconer's joints where they had been pulled and wrenched in the interrogations, back when Scorpius was a boy.

Richolf was a little slower to rise from his chair these days, took a little longer to get through his work, grimaced when he thought Scorpius wasn't looking. Another man his age wouldn't be so hobbled. But then most men Richolf's age had never tasted the full bitterness of the nobles' displeasure.

Turning the corner as though he'd not stopped to observe, Scorpius halted before Richolf and waited for instruction. His master seemed to block him out until he finished with his laborious knot. It gave Scorpius the ammunition he needed.

"Let me take that to the estate for you, sir."

Richolf merely glanced up at him in irritation.

He tried another tactic. "I know I don't drive as hard a bargain as you do."

"You don't drive any kind of bargain at all," his master said, smiling slightly.

"Just tell me what you mean to get for it, and I promise I won't leave without it."

Richolf braced himself and then rose to his feet. "I've got other supplies to get while I'm there," he said.

"Sir, you know I can get those for you."

His master sent him a sharp look, and Scorpius realized he'd done it again. It was just that Richolf was so stubborn. Sighing, he looked away so his master couldn't see his own frustration.

Richolf limped slowly to the door, gazing out at the downpour with his back to Scorpius. What could be so hard about collecting up an order of supplies, anyway? There must be some other business waiting for Richolf, something he couldn't —

Scorpius' face flushed with heat. Of course. How could he be so stupid? It must be Ingerith waiting for him. Of course it would be.

He looked over at his master with unspoken apologies. When Richolf faced him, Scorpius forced himself to meet his gaze. His master's expression changed from weariness to curiosity.

"I suppose you can't learn to drive a bargain if I don't send you to make one."

Relief and hope rose in Scorpius' chest. "I'll do my best, sir."

"You'd better," Richolf said. "Those traders will smell your inexperience and fall over themselves to fleece you."

Scorpius bit back what he'd nearly said. He was so close to being granted permission. Biting his lip, he squared his shoulders and waited.

"I'll draw up a list of provisions," Richolf said at last. "I want four hundred for the lot. Nothing less."

"Four hundred. Yes, sir," Scorpius said.

"As soon as this rain lets up, you may head out."

"Yes, sir. Thank you, sir."

Richolf eyes shadowed a little. "Let's put on the kettle. I could use a hot tea just now."

38

"Four hundred." Scorpius stared down the trader as if his heart wasn't beating a little too fast.

The weathered man's expression soured. "They aren't worth half that."

"You'd say that to my master's face, I suppose? And these are the same quality he always brings you. Four hundred." He'd already knocked it down from five-fifty. A promise to Richolf for four hundred was starting to sound less likely by the moment.

"Your master was drunk when he asked for such a figure."

The trader's derision shoved against Scorpius, chipping away at his resolve. Recalling Richolf's prediction that Scorpius would fail to drive a good bargain, he knew it was now or never.

"You know exactly who my master is. Who else brings you such pelts?" Scorpius forced himself to lean in and speak in a lower tone. The trader's brows knit together in confusion at first, but he cocked his head to listen.

"The truth is, my master trades here because it's closer for him," Scorpius said. "He has a hard time walking these days. Me, I don't have the same problem, do I? And there are three other estates a day's journey from here, all with markets, all with traders who'd love to get their hands on these inferior furs."

Scorpius stepped back and gave the trader time to make up his mind. The man was too experienced to give anything away, so Scorpius turned to gaze toward the gate and the road leading away from the estate. A hand upon his arm made him turn to the trader, who held out his other hand to shake on a deal.

"Four hundred," the trader said, and Scorpius made his first deal with a surge of pride flooding his chest. He helped the older man unload the pelts onto a cart, took the money and strolled away toward another market stall. There were a few items to purchase before he made his way back to the cottage.

He stopped short at the stall where he would find the little bells they needed for the falcon jesses.

The old woman who sold at this stall wasn't there this

morning. In her place was a girl about his own age, perhaps a little older. She was as fair as Scorpius was dark, with long honeyed curls cascading over her shoulders. An idiotic smile spread over his face before he could stop it.

The girl smirked, her eyes sparkling at his approach. "Good day," she said in a deeper voice than he would have imagined. He loved the richness of it.

"It's very good," he said, forcing his mouth to put away its grin. Yet it fought him.

"Is there something you're wanting this morning?" she said.

Scorpius could only gaze at her. He was certain she must think him a simpleton. "Bells," he said at last.

"Bells?" she asked. Her look of confusion — her slightly parted lips — were so charming that if she didn't stop he would have had to kiss her right there in front of the entire marketplace.

"For my birds," he said.

The girl's brow creased with annoyance, as though he were taunting her. Then she lit up with a smile of recognition. "Oh! You're the falconer's boy!"

Scorpius grinned again, far too widely for this simple trade at the seller's stall. He should take care that she didn't fleece him worse than he'd avoided with the pelt trader. He was in danger here.

A reckless joy made the possibilities intoxicating.

39

The girl stretched across the crowded market stall to take up a little covered woven basket. Enjoying the sight as she reached, Scorpius nearly missed his cue to look away in time.

The muffled sound of tiny bells beckoned from the container held in her palm. "Ma told me someone would stop by for these," she said, her eyes gleaming with mischief. "You… don't look anything like the man she described."

"Well, if I may say so," Scorpius said, waves of relief rolling through him at what he'd nearly said about the old woman before he knew it was her mother, "I nearly passed by this stall, as I was looking for someone other than yourself."

She grinned and dipped her head down in the most adorable manner. "You'll be wanting these, then?" Lifting the basket lid, she revealed several assortments of miniature bells held together by twine.

Scorpius leaned forward to peer inside just as the girl did likewise. They knocked heads.

"Ow!" she cried as the basket flew from her hand and bells scattered over the ground. Scorpius chuckled and bent to retrieve them when a grimy little boy darted from out of nowhere and scooped up a handful.

"Hey!" the girl shouted, shoving at Scorpius and reaching for the boy. He disappeared before Scorpius could blink.

One glance at the girl told him how great was her distress at the loss of her mother's wares. Scorpius bolted after the boy, scrambling to keep him in sight, darting and weaving between stalls and market goers.

It took a great deal of trouble, but Scorpius finally grabbed a handful of the boy's tunic. It nearly ripped in his hands, it was so threadbare. The feeling in his gut when the market girl had looked at him in despair was nothing compared to the chill in his heart when the beggar boy gazed into his eyes.

What a hard little person it was staring back at him, covered in grime and old scars, smelling to the heavens. No one to take him on as an apprentice, no one to care for him, no one but those he could steal from before they could give him a blow and a curse.

Still, these bells weren't his. He threw the boy down on the ground, pried his fingers open and retrieved the bells.

As he rose, panting, Scorpius noticed the boy hadn't run off as he'd supposed he might. Taking a moment to adjust his own tunic, he noticed the silent tears as the boy regained his feet. He also noticed how bony the boy's ankles were beneath ragged trousers.

Grabbing the boy by the shoulder, Scorpius saw the boy's instinctive flinch. Though his heart ached, Scorpius forced himself to remain gruff as he picked several bells from the retrieved loot and offered them back to the little thief.

The boy didn't give Scorpius time to change his mind. He scooped up the bells and took off, disappearing into the crowd.

Hardly anyone in the market had bothered to stop and look. Two boys fighting was hardly a matter for concern, especially when one was clearly a beggar. Scorpius made his way back to the girl's market stall, his heart soaring when he found her craning for a look at him.

He basked in her relief as he rejoined her, holding out the bells and dropping them back into her palm.

"Oh thank you!" she said, a catch in her voice. "Thank you!"

Scorpius shrugged as if all the running and jumping, the grabbing and sorting things out had been nothing at all.

"This is just the sort of thing Ma was saying would happen. She didn't want me to run the stall for her today, but she isn't well." Her voice thickened and she turned away.

So many tears today. Scorpius closed the space between them and said, "My master said the same thing. It's all turning out pretty much as he'd warned me."

She laughed and turned to smile up at him. Why did she look even prettier in the midst of her dismay? Was it the way she seemed to need him just now?

"I wish we didn't have to tell them they were right. Don't

you?" she said, wiping her face.

"You won't have to tell your ma anything. I'll buy the bells he made off with, as well as the ones I got back for you."

"Don't be silly." She shoved at him, but her face softened with hope.

"I'm not being anything except a terrible deal maker, just as my master predicted."

She swallowed and turned to someone stopping at her stall to make a purchase. When they'd finished their exchange, Scorpius moved to take his place, offering the money he would have paid for all of the bells.

"I can't," she said, shaking her head and smiling a warm and beautiful smile. She gasped as he took her hand and pressed the money upon her. "Your master won't let you near the market again if you're such a dreadful dealer."

"What would be the point of coming back, if your ma didn't let you run her stall for her?"

She laughed, a delightful sound that made him feel as though he'd performed the spirals and dives of a courting falcon.

40

When Scorpius rounded the curve in the road that revealed their cottage, the sight of his master sitting on a stool near the front door drew a smile, then a chuckle from him. Certainly, Richolf was busy polishing his boots. It was most definitely a fine day to sit outdoors and work.

The new hunting dog bounded up to greet him halfway along the road, trotting happily beside him as he approached the falconer.

"How did you fare?" Richolf asked, glancing up from his polishing.

Scorpius opened his leather satchel and retrieved the coins. He described his successful negotiations with the pelt trader, and explained to his master why he'd paid too much for the falcon jess bells.

"How much is left, then?" Richolf asked, his expression darkening more than Scorpius had expected.

When Scorpius told him the sum, his master put down his boots and stood, taking the money from Scorpius' hands with an abrupt swipe. Re-entering the cottage to secret away the coins, Richolf left Scorpius to stew alone.

For a moment, he considered picking up the boots and finishing the job for his master, but the unexpected reaction from Richolf stirred tight anger in Scorpius' chest. He'd only meant to spare his master the pain of the journey to the estate. Why should he act like Scorpius had done some terrible crime in helping out the market girl?

Striding quickly past the cottage, Scorpius headed for the falcon mews. He needed some time to cool down. He entered the dwelling of the hawk in need of the new bells, ignoring the raised wings and screech as the bird sensed his annoyance.

Scorpius grabbed the jesses from the hook and went outside to restring the bells. Just handling the delicate metal balls calmed him down, recalling the feel of the girl's palm as he returned them to her, following the chase after the little thief.

He would have thought Richolf would have approved of Scorpius coming to her aid. Apparently not. It was the sum of four hundred or nothing at all. Scorpius released the old bells and replaced them with the new ones, his anger merely simmering as he worked, not dissipating as he'd hoped.

No more was said of it until the time came to bring the next delivery of pelts to the estate market.

As Richolf counted up the furs and readied the bundle for the journey, Scorpius' heart swelled with hope that he would be granted permission to accompany his master. Oddly enough, his chest also squeezed with the echoes of anger. It wasn't fair, the way Richolf had responded to Scorpius' first efforts at trading in the marketplace.

Likely, he wouldn't be allowed to go. Scorpius mucked out the falcon mews with sharp movements, unable to believe his master could be so harsh.

He'd barely thought it when he remembered that night when the Nightmare Hunt had shown him what a cruel master really looked like. Giving a hot sigh, Scorpius stopped and leaned on the rake, just as Richolf entered the mews.

Scorpius started up with his work again, even though his shoulders ached, not wanting to make eye contact.

"I'll be needing you to take the pelts to market for me," Richolf said, as if he'd never yanked the coins from his grasp or insinuated that he'd made a poor trade.

"Sir?" Scorpius said, stopping his work and forcing himself to at least face his master, though he still avoided his gaze. His face burned hot with both the effort of raking and with unspoken words.

"You should be able to get five hundred for this lot."

"Five hundred," Scorpius said, nodding.

The memory of her face already lightened his heart. What if she wasn't there? What if it was her mother, returned to health and running the market stall?

No matter. She lived somewhere near the estate, or perhaps at the estate — he would soon discover where. The prospect of finding out her name drove the weariness from his muscles as he flew through the last of his chores.

41

"Five hundred?" the young trader said, laughing and turning away. "Get yourself another mug of ale. You're drunk."

Scorpius' face flushed hot, heart thudding with the desire to haul off and clobber the man. It didn't help that the pretty market girl watched from across the courtyard.

The older trader was absent, and he had no idea whether this one knew his master or not. His mind scrambled to come up with something that would give him leverage. Glancing down at the pelt bundle, he heard Richolf's assessment that this lot would command a price of five hundred.

So five hundred it would have to be.

Scorpius forged ahead with the dance of offer–counter-offer. The trader's mood rose and fell like gusts of wind. Scorpius had never seen anything quite like it. In the end he played upon the trader's quick temper. Like the red-tail swooping in for the kill, Scorpius saw his moment and dug his talons into the trader's latest offer.

The older trader would have been able to hold his decisions behind a mask, but this young trader had begun to sweat slightly. Scorpius knew he had him.

Thrusting his hand towards Scorpius, the trader said, "Four fifty."

Almost clasping his hand, Scorpius held back just in time. "No deal."

"You're a lunatic if you think that's worth more than four!"

"I know what I've got here, even if you're too full of yourself to admit it. The price for it is five. Take it or leave it."

The trader turned away, rubbing a hand over his face. Scorpius darted a glance over at the market stall. She was watching it all.

Standing straighter, Scorpius realized as if for the first time that he towered over the young man. He set his face into an expression which he hoped looked grim enough, in time to meet the trader's gaze.

There was real distress in the other man's eyes. "I'll give you four eighty. If you won't take that, I can't help you."

Scorpius hesitated. Five hundred, his master had said. Twenty was far more than the price of the stolen bells he'd spent without permission, and look what sort of reception that had received.

However, this trader was done. He had the same look of defeat that the game hens had in the clutches of the hawks. Extending his hand, Scorpius shook on the deal that soured both him and the trader. They exchanged goods for coin and parted without another word.

Trudging over to the market stall, he nearly forgot that the mere sight of the girl could mend things inside him so quickly. She turned and locked gazes with him. That was all it took.

Scorpius spent the afternoon standing beside her as she sold wares for her mother, who still wasn't well. He wasn't a great one for talking, but he listened as she told him all manner of things. The more she spoke, the more she giggled, and the bigger his heart seemed to swell in his chest. So strange.

He took a few bites of the food she'd brought with her, but only because she insisted that he had to eat something before his journey back to the cottage. Scorpius wasn't hungry for anything, only for the moments that flew by too quickly.

Finally, it was time to pack up the market stall. He insisted on helping her, though she protested she could do it and that he should go before he had to walk in the dark. When it was clear that she would only work herself into a knot if he didn't go on his way, Scorpius began walking toward the gates that led from the estate.

Turning, he said, "You know, I don't think you've told me your name."

She bit her lip but couldn't prevent a delightful smile from spreading over her face. "I'm Alegreza."

"Alegreza," he said, returning her grin. "I'm Scorpius."

"Scorpius," she said, with the same tone of wonder he'd used.

"Give my best to your ma," he said.

"Good luck with your master," she said.

He nodded, a little worm of dread squirming through his gut. Scorpius shook it off, forcing himself to walk through the estate entrance and head for the cottage as the sun dipped below the horizon and shadows cooled the road.

When he finally opened the door and came in from the chilly evening, he took a deep breath to steady himself. Richolf would surely have something to say about the price he'd failed to get for the pelts.

His master looked up from where he sat at the table, eating his dinner. "I was starting to wonder whether you'd be back tonight."

"The time got away from me," Scorpius said.

"Well don't just stand there. Fix yourself something to eat." Richolf bit into his bread.

Scorpius still wasn't hungry. His stomach twisted as he worried about the money he hadn't secured. Filling his plate anyway, he sat and looked at the food, not eating, not speaking.

"Scorpius," his master said finally.

"Sir?" he said, not looking up.

"Is there something you want to tell me?"

Reaching down for the leather bag heavy with coins, Scorpius handed it over to his master. Richolf hefted the weight of it.

"How much did you get for it?"

Forcing himself to answer, his hands icy, his mouth dry, Scorpius said, "Four eighty."

Placing the bag on the table, Richolf continued to eat. Scorpius stared at his master, his heart still beating hard in readiness for harsh words. None came.

Picking up his fork, Scorpius stabbed and missed at a piece of meat. They ate in silence for a few moments, but the dog's eyebrows furrowed with the unspoken tension in the air.

"Couldn't get five hundred for it," Richolf finally said.

"No, sir." *Here it comes*, Scorpius thought.

"Not surprised," his master said.

"I tried my best, sir." Scorpius flushed hot.

"And you did well." Richolf's eyes sparkled with a private joke.

"I did?"

Richolf took a long swig from his tankard. "Those pelts were only worth four hundred."

42

Scorpius strode through the gates of the courtyard, his gaze immediately seeking the market stall where Alegreza sold her ma's wares. The cobblestones lay bare beside the stall where one could purchase leather from the tanner.

Perhaps it would have been wiser to inquire about the market girl right away. Scorpius forged ahead with selling the pelt bundle, even though his mind was far from the business at hand.

"Would you know that market girl who sells trinkets?" he asked as the old trader counted the coins and passed them to Scorpius.

"Alegreza?"

"Yes, that's the one." A murmur of unease rustled in Scorpius' mind at the look on the trader's face.

"Her ma died, poor thing."

"I wondered," Scorpius said, gazing at the missing market stall.

The trader turned to be on his way.

"Ah, would you ... do you know where, ah ... ?" Scorpius stammered.

Not smiling exactly, the trader said, "You'll find her in the room above the clothier's."

Nodding as though he might have the slightest inkling where he might find such a place, Scorpius waited until the trader was gone before pointing himself in the direction of the more permanent row of buildings at the edge of the courtyard. He strolled slowly and carefully past all of them before he encountered one that held bolts of brightly-colored cloth and an excitable man gesturing instructions to his apprentice.

Gazing up, he noticed a second story above this place with a small window.

Well, best go in and ask whether this was the place or not.

"By all means," the clothier said in an irritated tone. "Perhaps you can do something with her. She's got until tomorrow before I call the bailiff to remove her from my premises. I have another family who can pay, and the room is theirs the day after tomorrow. So, please."

He swept an arm to indicate the ladder propped against a hole in the ceiling. Scorpius nodded his thanks and climbed up into the dim interior.

Alegreza's sniffles filled the tiny, barren room, reaching into his gut and yanking without warning.

"Afternoon," he said softly, and her expression almost broke him. She folded into his embrace as he slid by her side and knelt, wrapping his arms around her. Scorpius rocked her, her choked cries reminding him of a day long ago when a falconer had come to fetch him from the nursery. He hadn't cried that day, but he'd wanted to.

It didn't take too much convincing before he'd tugged her to her feet, helped her to pack her few things in a bundle and climb down the ladder. A brief scuffle ensued as the clothier attempted to stop Alegreza from leaving before her rent was paid.

At her renewed tears and pale despair, Scorpius blocked the clothier from reaching her, barking at her to leave.

"I demand my money!" the clothier said. "This is not a charity house!"

For the briefest of moments, Scorpius thought of the coins weighing his master's purse in his own satchel. Then he remembered the way Richolf had grabbed the remainder of the sum when Scorpius had overpaid Alegreza for the stolen bells.

Stepping towards the clothier, who was also a tall man but slender, Scorpius copied the manner of that cruel lord from the Night of Screams. "Have you no feeling?" he said, his voice squeaking as it did without warning these days.

"Don't think I don't know who you are, falconer's boy." The clothier stepped even closer, standing nose to nose with him. "I shall pay your master a visit and see where my missing rent has gone."

Gazing down at the clothier's slippered feet, Scorpius said,

"Don't forget, it's half a day's walk. Until then," and he forced himself to bow slightly.

Collecting the market girl and heading out onto the road, Scorpius felt a surge of excitement swirling through the worry about Richolf, the disputed rent and his lack of permission to bring this girl to his master's cottage. The heady thrill made his long legs bolt too quickly, and Scorpius kept backtracking to catch up with Alegreza's distracted pace.

As she was clearly in no mood for conversation, Scorpius left his whirlpool of questions unspoken. Instead, they walked most of the way in silence. They passed a small cluster of grazers driven by a shepherd with a fierce gaze that missed nothing. Glancing at Alegreza, Scorpius realized she'd stopped crying and was grateful to the shepherd for providing a distraction.

Rounding the bend towards the cottage, Scorpius smiled at the dog's breakneck welcome as he barreled towards them. Alegreza huddled behind him, so Scorpius coaxed her to let the dog near for her scent.

Satisfied that she was friend and not foe, the dog bounded back to the cottage, where Richolf stood waiting in the doorway. A chill of nerves washed through Scorpius. After all, this cottage was where he lived but it did not belong to him. He had no right whatsoever to offer shelter to anyone.

As they neared, he tried to think of all the things he might say to sway his master into accepting the market girl for even one night. Yet his mind was empty of words, still full of the memory of Alegreza sitting alone in the nearly-empty room.

They stood before Richolf, who took a long look at the two of them before standing aside so they could walk through the door.

43

Scorpius melted at the look of delight on her face when she saw the tiny bells from her ma's market stall, now tinkling on the leg of the red-tail. Stretching his arm toward the hawk, Scorpius waited for the bird to mount his gauntleted perch. As much as he wanted to show Alegreza what he did out here at the falconer's cottage, there was no hurrying a hawk.

The dog trotted happily beside him on one side, Scorpius keenly wishing it could be Alegreza. Skittish around animals, she lagged behind.

He led the way out to the field and began the hunt, explaining every aspect of it to her, relishing her focused attention, the way she noted everything as though he meant for her to apprentice along with him. For a heady moment, as he watched her follow the trajectory of the hawk as it soared after something in the tall grasses, Scorpius wondered if there had ever been such a thing as a girl for a falconer's apprentice.

As though someone had taken a swing at him, Scorpius' head rocked backward as he remembered the screams of the slave girls running naked across this very field, chased down by the lords in the torchlight.

He shook his head to clear the memory, but his hands shook and his breath came in shudders. Distracted by the hunt, Alegreza seemed oblivious to his sudden distress. At least, if she noticed, she didn't let on.

It struck him hard that the falconer's cottage was no place for her. Richolf would be glad that he'd come to this bit of truth on his own. Yet it didn't stop Scorpius' heart from weighing heavily in his chest.

When she turned to gaze up at him, a mix of wonder and dismay in her eyes at the skill of the hawk as it took down the game, Scorpius was seized inside with too many feelings bursting up from his gut. He dropped his satchel and grabbed Alegreza by the arms. Before he knew what he was doing, his lips covered hers.

She stiffened, so Scorpius pulled away, letting go of her arms to cover his mouth with his hand, as though he could retrieve what had already escaped. Forcing his scrambled mind to snap back into place, he gave the order to the dog to find the downed game. Bending low to pick up his abandoned satchel, he thought ahead to the next part of this demonstration, wishing he hadn't brought her out here, not wanting to speak to her, or look at her, or be this close to her.

Alegreza crouched beside him, helping to gather his things. He stopped and gazed at her.

She was still grieving her mother, the loss darkening her eyes. He'd brought her out here because she had no place else to go. She must feel as trapped as he'd felt that day, so many years ago, when Nurse had released him and he'd been forced to follow the falconer to this strange place.

They gathered everything in silence, following the dog to the kill.

When they'd collected a small brace of game, Scorpius led them back to the cottage so they could prepare the meat for roasting. It went so much quicker with Alegreza nearly taking command of the kitchen. His master exchanged amused looks with Scorpius as they worked.

Assuring them that she could finish the meal, Alegreza all but chased them outside while she bustled about inside the cottage. Richolf stepped out into the cool evening, stretching his stiff limbs and turning to Scorpius.

"I know, sir," Scorpius said first. "I know she can't stay."

Nodding, Richolf let that settle for a moment. Then he said, "I'll send word to Ingerith. She may know of a position for her."

The crush of worry over Alegreza lightened inside him. Ingerith. Why hadn't he thought of that?

Scorpius settled in to wait for the call to step inside the falconer's own cottage. The dog pressed against his legs, so he rubbed him absently.

The fact that he had no idea where his master's lover actually lived, and that all communication between them had to be done in the strictest of confidences, drew a new slither of worry along Scorpius' spine. Surely Ingerith would never deliver Alegreza into the hands of a master as cruel as the lord who'd organized that terrible hunt.

He thought of the whole crowd of them, cheering one another on as they each took down a slave girl, ladies applauding as well as lords. He had to believe there were some nobles who didn't murder their brothers on the falconer's front steps, or rip open a young guard's back for displaying common humanity.

Somewhere there had to be a noble house where the market girl could serve, have a bed and food and not have to fear being grabbed for a kiss as Scorpius had grabbed and kissed her in the field.

44

She took him by surprise, her slender fingers cupping his face before he could catch his breath.

His eyes widened with shock, only to see her lashes closing before him, too near to focus. He stiffened as she had done, but when her lips covered Scorpius', he kissed her back.

She'd caught him on his knees, twisting back from securing the replacement perch in one of the hawk mews. When he wrapped his arms around her, she pulled back to gaze down at him.

The look in her eyes left no doubt that she desired him. His confusion must have played over his face, because she traced the line of his eyebrows with delicate concern.

"Alegreza," he said. Placing one finger on his mouth, she shook her head solemnly.

A deep shiver of delight ran its way through Scorpius at the way she gazed at him. He could forget all about the way she'd huddled by herself in her ma's empty room above the clothier's shop. Her eyes weren't shadowed by grief, weren't shimmering with the tears which had raked across his heart every time they rolled down her face.

Now she radiated command, as though her entire life wasn't dependent upon whether the falconer's secret lover could find a position for her to serve at an estate. It made his heart swell to see her gaze down at him like this.

He was just covering her hands with his own, intending to kiss them, when his master's voice rang out in the distance. Scorpius made to gain his feet, but Alegreza pressed down hard on his shoulders.

Glancing up in irritation, he wasn't prepared for the flood of longing that rushed through him at her silent order to keep quiet. She slowly shook her head, *no,* raising bumps all over his skin.

Richolf's voice grew closer. Scorpius couldn't stop himself from moving to answer several times, but she held him like a hunter holding back a dog. Eventually his master went searching for him elsewhere.

"What—?" he asked, grabbing her wrist as if to shake her off.

"Isn't this what you wanted?" she said. "The other day, in the field?"

He nodded, swallowing hard.

"Well, I want it, too." She slipped her arm from his grasp, once again taking hold of his face, which made his heart thump in anticipation. "And if I'm to go to an estate to serve, I can't wait for things to happen someday."

It weighed heavily inside him, the image of her departure haunting his mind's eye.

When Richolf's voice called out again, he looked up into the market girl's eyes and saw her determination to seize this moment while she was still mistress of herself.

He'd never openly disobeyed his master before. If he'd done anything wrong, it was because he hadn't understood something or had acted in error. Right now, hiding in the mews with Alegreza, Scorpius too felt the need to reach for a little piece of his own joy.

Grabbing her tightly to him, Scorpius kissed her deeply, so deeply she sagged to her knees to join him.

45

Scorpius grabbed at her skirt as she rose, but Alegreza darted just out of reach. Her giggle filled the secluded grove where the last bites of a delicious meal remained on the cloth spread beneath the trees.

Richolf and Ingerith already clapped a merry tune, so Scorpius joined in as Alegreza danced for them. Ingerith hummed and Alegreza spun, her quick little feet tapping an irresistible rhythm.

She flashed her legs now and then with a deft twist of her hands upon her skirts, shooting glances at Scorpius that sent the heat to his face. Ingerith got the same looks, however, so they must be a part of the dance. Still, an odd feeling came over him that his master and his master's lover should be witness to them.

When she finished, everyone clapped and laughed in delight. Alegreza flopped down on the forest floor beside him, catching her breath. She glanced at him but looked to Ingerith, who nodded.

Richolf rose slowly to his feet as his old injuries protested. "I feel like a walk just now," he said, catching Scorpius' eye.

Indeed, the two women bent their heads together in whispered conversation. Scrambling awkwardly to his feet, Scorpius joined his master along the path which had brought them here for this dreamlike afternoon.

"Are they...?" Scorpius said.

Nodding, Richolf left it at that until they were well out of hearing range. Then he stopped short and looked Scorpius squarely in the eye. "I know it's all happening rather quickly," he said.

Scorpius' stomach knotted up. "Ingerith found a position for her."

The expression on his master's face did nothing to reassure Scorpius. "She may have. Everything depends upon the patron, and whether Alegreza is suitable."

Fear for the market girl reared up in Scorpius' chest, scattering the laughter of their outing like a whirlwind. Words and questions caught in his throat, words he dare not speak. If he remained silent, the images that sprang to his mind might yet be beaten back.

"In a few days time, a noble will come to us for a hunt," Richolf said. "He will also collect Alegreza — if she pleases him."

Scorpius turned away, the memory of his master's lover in the arms of another man blinding him. All of the secrecy, the notes passed through third parties, Ingerith's threats that she would discover the names of the men responsible for torturing her beloved — all of it made sense in a flood of clarity.

"Does she know?" he said. "Does she understand where she would be going?"

"She already knows," Richolf said sadly.

"There's nothing else she could do?" Scorpius said, his voice tight with emotion. "Did Ingerith even inquire?"

"She wouldn't make this offer lightly." A tone of warning rose in his master's voice.

Scorpius ignored it. The hammering of his pulse drove all caution from his mind. "I can inquire, sir. Let me go to the estate."

"I told you, she's aware of the offer." Richolf's face darkened.

The remains of Alegreza's kisses clung to Scorpius' skin, driving him to blurt out, "Sir, you're not giving her a chance!"

His master grabbed him roughly by the arms, pulling him close. "What sort of chance do you think she'd have if she was a housemaid? You don't remember what it was like for those slave girls they brought out here?"

Scorpius returned Richolf's burning gaze. "I do remember, sir. Yet you send her to the very same fate, only in finer clothing."

Richolf shoved him away so that Scorpius stumbled and nearly lost his footing. "Ingerith enjoys some portion of power over herself. That is more than most penniless market girls with no family could hope for. So you would do well to thank Ingerith for going through the considerable trouble to procure this patron for Alegreza."

Biting back more words, Scorpius nodded, his helplessness burning behind his eyes. He, too, had no family, only a master with a courtesan for a lover.

46

When Alegreza left, Scorpius stood beside Richolf, somehow pulling together the appearance of an obedient apprentice. He didn't know how he managed to make himself stand there, suddenly sick to death of suppressing his every desire in order to serve, always serve.

It was in that nearly imperceptible moment before Richolf turned to say something to him that did it. Scorpius watched that little hitch in his master's shoulders that told him Richolf, too, had to gather himself up in order to do something that he didn't want to do.

It all boiled over inside of Scorpius. He couldn't bear to have his master look at him, to have him say the words he'd have to dredge up from somewhere deep, deep down inside of him. Scorpius spun on his heel and made to bolt away from this hideous ache in his chest.

Richolf yanked him to an awkward halt.

For a split second, Scorpius nearly threw his master off. Fighting to control himself, he kept his gaze from meeting Richolf's.

"Oh no, you don't," Richolf said, pulling him close.

Scorpius stiffened, looking at the empty bend in the road.

"You are not going to ruin her chance for a good life," his master said, squeezing his arm and shaking him slightly.

"Please stop saying that." Scorpius heard the catch in his voice, hating the undisguised sense of futility in his voice.

"There are too many things you don't understand."

"Are there?" Scorpius dare not look at Richolf now. The fury that built inside him was too wild. If his master kept patronizing him, Scorpius wouldn't be able to crush it all back any longer.

Richolf loosened his grip slightly. "Believe me, Scorpius. If there is anyone who knows how you feel…"

Scorpius couldn't bear it. He wrenched free, looking at his master in time to see the shock on Richolf's face. Thrusting his arms forward with all his considerable strength, Scorpius pinned his master against the cottage.

"Why? Did your master sign Ingerith up? Is that how it's done?" Scorpius' anger didn't soften the stab of regret coiling through his gut.

He shouldn't treat his master this way. He let Richolf go and took a step back.

Before he could blink, Richolf grabbed hold of him, switching places to slam Scorpius face-first into the stone cottage wall. Scorpius grunted, his master's grip on his twisted arm forcing him to squirm.

"I won't have any comments like that from you about her, is that clear?" Richolf said in the most chilling voice.

Icy dread dribbled down Scorpius' spine. He nodded, barely stifling a cry as Richolf shoved him painfully against the cottage, the pressure on his arm close to the breaking point.

"Of all people, Ingerith deserves better than what she's endured," Richolf said. "You think I'm going to stand here and listen to your judgement upon her? Do you?"

Scorpius pressed his forehead against the cool stone, breathing deeply to bear the pain.

"I understand how you're feeling, Scorpius. I've been wrestling with those same exact feelings every day, since before I brought you here from the nursery."

"Just because you're used to it doesn't mean it should be this way."

His master let him go. Turning as quickly as he could, Scorpius kept Richolf squarely in his sights.

"No," his master said, eyes dark with warning. "It shouldn't be this way. No one should have left you at the nursery, either — if you were an embarrassing reminder of an unseemly affair, why raise you to be a noble if they were going to hand you over to someone like me?"

His master's words drove a dagger of pain to scrape against Scorpius' heart.

"I have tried to shield you, Scorpius. There's enough misery waiting for you out there. I tried to make your life here as good as I could make it. There's only so much a falconer can do."

All Scorpius could see in his mind's eye was his Alegreza stretching out upon a bed before the gaze of a noble. He swallowed thickly against the sick feeling that threatened to choke him.

Richolf shook his head. "Shielding you — it's turned around to haunt us both. How can you entertain thoughts that this world is in any way fair? Where did that come from?"

Scorpius straightened as tall as he could. "Can't imagine, sir."

Richolf's eyes narrowed at Scorpius' tone. "You will speak to me with respect."

Though his stomach felt like he'd taken a punch, Scorpius fought the urge to bow his head. "Sir."

"Get inside before I lose what's left of my temper."

Darting a glance at the empty bend in the road, Scorpius felt Alegreza's absence like a severed limb. With heavy steps, he turned and made his way through the door of the cottage.

He stood unseeing before the sideboard. Everything felt like a nightmare. Nothing made sense anymore.

According to his master, he should be grateful that his sweetheart was heading for the arms of a noble. And why not? That's how his master's lover made her way through life, through this unfair life full of cruelly-used slave girls and abandoned market girls. To the nobles, they were all game hens, anyway, weren't they? Flapping madly in a doomed bid for life, while the hawks calmly climbed to that sweet spot in midair before diving in for the kill.

47

He did not have leave to go to the estate. His master kept him on a tight leash, and Scorpius chafed against it. Their meals together were brief, tense affairs, their daily work separate, their places at the hunt on opposite ends of the field.

Scorpius was grateful when a young noble was paired with him on a warm morning. Generally he preferred talking as little as possible with the lords, but things had been so silent between himself and Richolf lately.

He found he could make the noble laugh easily, and in turn laughed at the lord's wry take on things. He was close in age to Scorpius, after all. If things had worked out differently for him, the noble may very well have been a friend.

As the hunt wound down, the sweat plastered Scorpius' tunic to his back. Lord Thibault undid the laces of his hunting doublet and slipped out of it, his fine linen shirt soaked.

"I'm for a swim," he said, gazing about him. "Where do you hide away a spot for that?"

Gesturing towards the cottage, Scorpius said, "We bathe in the stream closer to the cottage."

"Show me!" and the noble took off at a run.

Scorpius hadn't fully tied together the brace of hens yet. He couldn't very well leave them, yet the young lord was already well ahead and dashing in the wrong direction.

With the same sense of reckless disregard for a lifetime of obedience sparked by his time with the market girl, Scorpius dropped the game hens onto the grass and tore after the noble. A surge of power fed his limbs as he caught up to the lord and then overtook him.

"This way!" he called and dashed into the trees toward the flat rock and the deep bend in the stream. Lord Thibault put on a burst of speed now that he had clear direction. The two ran abreast, weaving between trees, crashing through branches and laughing with the joy of it.

With the stream in clear view, Scorpius pulled back on

his momentum. Lord Thibault burst into the clearing a few strides in the lead, a wide grin lighting his face as he turned, victorious, towards Scorpius.

"You let me win," the noble said, still smiling as he peeled off his clothes.

"No, my lord," Scorpius said, catching his breath and shedding his own clothes.

Lord Thibault waded into the cool water and flopped backwards, splashing Scorpius who was close behind him. He slipped beneath the surface, welcoming this relief against his sticky skin.

The young noble popped up, grabbing hold of Scorpius and dunking him. If it had been Richolf, Scorpius would have grabbed and dunked his opponent in return.

Yet whatever happened, Scorpius must not lay hands upon the young lord. Instead he must choke on water and try not to drown. Lord Thibault hauled him up and looked him squarely in the eye.

Scorpius returned his gaze for a long moment before looking down. He should not have done it — he knew that — but something about this young noble insisted upon tossing protocol aside.

"I detest being lied to," Lord Thibault said.

Scorpius said nothing, merely watched the surface of the water settle before him.

"If I was not your better, would you have reached the stream before me?" the noble asked.

A spear of danger pierced the space between them. Scorpius must not forget what the nobles were capable of doing to those who served them. His heart chilling inside him, Scorpius gathered his courage and said, "Yes, my lord."

He stole a glance at Lord Thibault, who struggled to hide both disappointment and satisfaction from showing on his face. "Have you served out here very long?" he asked, stretching backwards in the water.

"Since I was fetched from the nursery, my lord." It was not to be spoken of, his suspect parentage. Yet the words had escaped.

Lord Thibault froze, kneeling in the water to meet Scorpius' gaze. "What do you mean?"

"I mean only that I was brought up at the manor house nursery not far from here, my lord."

"What are you doing out here, then?" The young noble's brow furrowed with concern.

Scorpius tried to speak, but his throat choked with unspoken words finally emerging. "No one... no one ever... no one ever came for me, you see. Only the falconer."

Lifting his gaze to stare deeply into the young noble's eyes, Scorpius saw an echo of the horror he'd always crushed down at his abandonment. "Nurse released me to him. So I became his apprentice. And I've served here ever since. My lord."

"Imagine it," Lord Thibault said in a hushed tone.

Scorpius held his breath and slid down beneath the water, letting the coolness engulf him. He had to collect himself before returning to his master. The anger that consumed him at Alegreza's treatment propelled Scorpius into saying and doing things he never would have considered only weeks before.

And though he now wished he could stay submerged here beneath the surface of the stream, the rippling image of Lord Thibault reminded him that he must resurface, even if his burning lungs did not.

48

The following week, Lord Thibault arrived with his retinue, sweeping up to the falconer's cottage on his charger which flashed with silver ornament. Richolf dropped his work, standing to greet them.

Scorpius trotted to join Richolf in time to see the noble brush past his master, instead heading straight for him.

"There you are!" Lord Thibault said, face erupting into a smile.

Scorpius bowed, his face heating at Richolf's look of shock.

"I've had an abysmal week," the noble said, forcing Scorpius to hurry along beside him as he headed toward the field. "Couldn't wait to get back here for a hunt. Just the thing, eh?"

Scorpius darted a glance back at his master, whose expression darkened. "Apologies, my lord," he said. "Shouldn't we collect up a falcon, at least?"

"Oh, he'll see to it, won't you?" the noble said to Richolf.

"Certainly, my lord," the falconer said, bowing with a sidelong glare that shot a chill through Scorpius. Shaking it off, he passed by the mews with their hawks perched in the shadows. To be dragged ahead like this, with nothing to be done but obey the young lord gave Scorpius a strange sensation of freedom from the chokehold which Richolf had lately placed upon him.

Lord Thibault's guard stood at a respectful distance, his courtiers remaining with Richolf as Scorpius entertained the young lord. Making their lethal dives, the falcons took out the game hens that Scorpius' master coaxed from cover. An odd afternoon indeed.

"I can't tell you what a relief it is to come out here," Lord Thibault said as the hunt began to wind down.

At first, Scorpius started to answer as he would to any noble.

Yet there was something in the young lord's tone, something in the way he kept looking at him. Perhaps Scorpius should beware. Perhaps that's what his master's expression had been, earlier — a warning to be careful, and not the outrage of being made to serve his own apprentice.

"Are you troubled, my lord?"

The young noble glanced quickly at Scorpius, fixing him with an appraising stare that made Scorpius suspect his master had indeed been sending him a warning. After a long moment, Lord Thibault chuckled. "I dare say I have a dominion's worth of trouble."

"We're pleased to offer this small consolation, then."

"You know, ever since our last conversation, well... frankly, I've been dreaming about what it would have been like to have never been collected up from the nursery, as you were not."

Scorpius looked at Lord Thibault, trying to gauge the young man's mood before looking away in time to avoid eye contact. The noble gazed out over the woods, lost in troubled thought.

"Surely not, my lord," Scorpius said finally.

"Do you even know what's brewing?" Lord Thibault asked. He turned and looked at Scorpius as though the lighthearted noble who had arrived earlier had been merely a front for the sake of his companions.

Wishing he could dart a glance at his master for any kind of sign or direction, Scorpius took a breath, gathered himself and made his choice. "Can't say that I do, my lord."

Nodding his head toward Richolf, the noble said, "Wonder if he knows, and he just hasn't told you."

It was Scorpius' turn to chuckle. "That would be just like him, my lord."

"Really. Perhaps our masters aren't very different after all."

Hearing this noble try to bridge the gap between them made Scorpius' heart ache with such unexpected force that he took a step back.

"Well, I shall tell you a little something, then. Something your master should know, if he doesn't already."

"My lord." Scorpius looked into Lord Thibault's eyes, surprised to see the depth of weariness suddenly exposed.

"The Troubles have begun." Lord Thibault's voice caught as he said it. He blinked rapidly and looked away.

49

It all made sense now.

His master had not glared at him when Lord Thibault swept Scorpius to the hunt, leaving the rest of his retinue behind. That look had been a warning, the only kind permitted between a falconer and his apprentice.

Beware.

Suddenly Scorpius' hands shook. His master seemed so very far away across the field, rather than not far enough.

Lord Thibault swiped a hand across his face, turning to gaze at Scorpius. It no longer seemed possible that they were close in age, not with the weight that seemed to bear down upon the noble.

Memories tumbled forward, stopping Scorpius' breath.

They jumbled through his mind — a noble's rod slicing the back of Scorpius' head, the lords fighting on the doorstep, the sword plunging into the royal brother. They were all part of The Troubles, weren't they?

Across the field, Richolf appeared to be calmly collecting the braces of game, but he was staring over at Scorpius. Was he trying to tell him something, give him some further warning?

His master still carried the wounds from those days and nights of torture. He'd been put to the question because the royal brothers had decided the falconer's cottage was tucked away enough to settle their score out here. Nothing to do with the falconer, and yet his body held the torment even now.

Of course, not even that could compare to the Hunt of Screams.

Scorpius met Lord Thibault's gaze, suddenly angered by the noble's tears. "The Troubles, my lord?" he said, his voice tight as he fought to control himself. "Yes they've made their presence known, even to those who try to live apart from them."

Once again, instead of taking offense to such a tone from a falconer's boy, Lord Thibault dropped his reserve even lower. "Am I in danger here?" he asked plainly, staring deeply into

Scorpius' eyes.

Glancing over at his master, he saw his attempts to gather the courtiers and head from the field. Yet there were two laggards.

Scorpius busied himself with his own braces of game. "My master warns of it, my lord."

Lord Thibault started to turn, to look toward the others.

"Don't!" Scorpius hissed.

The noble froze.

"Carry on as you would, my lord," Scorpius ordered, not caring that he did so. He risked another glance as he crouched to tie the games hens together. Those two courtiers bent their heads together. More to the point, one glanced in Lord Thibault's direction.

"We must run for it." Scorpius stopped his work but remained in position. "Will you do it?"

He wished he could look at Lord Thibault, but doing so now would plunge the knife in.

"Where do we go?" the noble said, his voice calmer now that it had come to this.

"They are in my forest, my lord. I know these trees, I know the hills, and they do not. Just follow me."

Scorpius rose, leaving the brace of game and catching Lord Thibault's eye. At his nod, they bolted toward the tree line. Just as they reached cover, the noble lost his footing and grunted. Scorpius turned to see Lord Thibault scramble up and shake it off, his face drained of color.

Slipping between the trees, Scorpius ran as Lord Thibault kept pace beside him. He listened hard, but it was a good while before he made out their pursuers. They had a chance to reach the hiding place that would protect them.

The lord's breathing was labored. Glancing over at Lord Thibault, Scorpius saw the arrow shaft protruding from the noble's shoulder. Speckles of blood dribbled from his mouth onto his hunting doublet.

Branches snapped loudly behind them. There was nothing

else he could do. Grabbing Lord Thibault by the arms, he swung him around and onto his knees.

Eyes screwing shut with the pain, Lord Thibault stayed silent as Scorpius dragged him down and on top of himself, under a boulder ledge gripped hard by gnarled roots. They lay there panting in the gray light, yet quiet enough as their pursuers charged past them deeper into the forest.

Scorpius steeled himself to ignore the drops of blood that fell onto his cheek as Lord Thibault fought for breath. He remembered how safe he'd felt when his master had shielded him under a rock ledge very much like this one. Dragons or nobles, it was all the same.

Reaching up, he wrapped his fingers around the lord's arm and squeezed a quick message. Lord Thibault passed out a heartbeat later.

50

Scorpius ran with stealthy assurance back towards the hunting field. Lord Thibault was safely hidden beneath the rock ledge, though he couldn't be sure the noble truly understood the instructions Scorpius had whispered to him.

No time to worry about that. He had to fetch his master to mend the noble, or there would be more lords descending upon this place, and they would demand crushing retribution.

It was already possible that Lord Thibault wouldn't make it through this. Scorpius shoved that idea far from his mind. The noble could not die. He would not allow it.

His master could never survive another round of being put to the question.

And what was to stop them from dragging Scorpius to the same fate? Was he not the servant who'd tried to shield Lord Thibault?

Scorpius' footfalls padded softly through the forest, but his breathing sounded so loud, ricocheting off the trees. Darting glances showed no pursuers, but he felt the danger raking across his skin.

The light in the forest grew as he neared the field's edge. It revealed two bodies splayed between fallen logs.

Checking his speed, heart hammering in fear, Scorpius glanced down to see the fine courtiers' clothes marred with blood. His master was not among these.

Bursting from the cover of the forest, Scorpius saw another tangle of bodies among the tall grasses. The dog lay close to one of them.

Scorpius' heart shot through with a sickening dread. For a moment he couldn't bear to move.

A groan wove its way into the sunshine. Forcing himself to walk forward, Scorpius found his master curled onto his side. The dog's nose was tucked into the little space between Richolf's neck and the trampled field.

Dropping to his knees, Scorpius checked his master quickly

for wounds.

"I'll live," croaked Richolf, rolling onto his back.

"Are there any others here?" Scorpius said, rubbing the dog whose tail wagged uncertainly.

"Two have not returned," Richolf said, sitting up painfully. "They were after you."

Scorpius gazed into his master's eyes, almost unable to meet the worry that burned there. Bowing his head, Scorpius started to say how sorry he was, but his master interrupted him.

Cupping Scorpius' face with his rough hands, Richolf said, "Where is Lord Thibault?"

Assured that he was well hidden, Richolf rose to his knees, surveying the field, scanning the forest's edge for any signs of the courtiers' return.

"You'll need to fetch him."

"How, sir? He cannot walk."

"We'll get him out on horseback."

Scorpius nodded, but his heart sank. He'd never ridden a horse in his life. And the young lord's mount was a spirited, powerful animal.

Glancing again at his master, at the scars that had never faded on the falconer's hands and neck, Scorpius knew he would do whatever it took to keep Richolf from the torments.

Which was easier said than done, as he rounded the corner of the cottage and saw Lord Thibault's horse challenging him with raised head and suspicious black eye.

51

Lord Thibault's stallion barely tolerated Scorpius' efforts to hang onto the reins, and that was merely to lead him to Richolf on the field.

The guard who'd sprawled nearby had regained consciousness. He rolled the still-bleeding courtier facedown and secured his hands behind his back as Scorpius helped his master into the saddle.

"We'll secure the grounds," the guard said, nodding at another guard who had already rounded up two courtiers farther along the field. "Bring his lordship to your cottage."

"Aye, sir," Richolf said, reaching down to grab hold of Scorpius' forearm. The horse side-stepped in a circle, forcing Scorpius to hop on one leg until finally Richolf hauled him up. Perching on the thoroughbred's bare haunches, he wrapped his arms around Richolf and hung on, grateful beyond measure that he didn't need to ride this beast by himself.

This forest was Richolf's before it was Scorpius', so a brief description was all it took for his master to pick their way through the dense growth. Scorpius stayed on the alert for the two courtiers who'd chased Lord Thibault and himself into these woods, but the only sounds were birdsong and rustling from small, skittish creatures.

When they finally closed in on the rock ledge sheltering the noble, the horse's ears pricked forward as it sniffed the air. Scorpius slid off and helped Richolf down, seeing the blood caked in his hair for the first time.

Crawling beneath the gnarled tree roots gripping the rock, Scorpius found Lord Thibault insensible but breathing. Between himself and his master, they eased the noble from his hiding place and onto the horse with silent signals and practiced understanding, but not before stuffing a neckcloth in the lord's mouth to stop the moaning.

Picking their way as carefully and quickly as they could, Richolf supported Lord Thibault from his seat behind him on the horse as Scorpius managed the animal with greater assurance. There was no time for anything else.

By the time they made their way to the field, there was nothing but mashed grass to indicate that anything had even happened here. Scorpius and his master exchanged grim glances as they headed along the mews, forcing themselves to ignore the falcon perched on the roof of his hut, untended after the hunt.

Rounding the corner of the cottage, Scorpius saw four courtiers tied to the hitching posts, some faint with their wounds, some glaring in dark warning. One injured guard stood over them, his blade at the ready.

The other hurried to assist Lord Thibault into the cottage. Scorpius had to secure the horse, though he still didn't know what he was doing. All he knew was that the animal responded better when Scorpius acted as if he knew what was what. So that's what he did. He ignored the size and power and aggressive temperament and treated the stallion as though he were their hunting dog.

When he finally entered the kitchen, he found Lord Thibault laid upon his stomach on the table, the arrow still protruding from his shoulder. The guard deftly probed with his fingers, moving the shaft this way and that until he was satisfied as to the placement of the arrowhead. Richolf held the noble down and jerked his head for Scorpius to do the same.

The guard rummaged through his leather satchel for a few items, asked for water and some cloths and wiped the sweat from his brow. Scorpius scurried to collect what he required. By the time he returned, the guard had collected himself and readied the small knife and clamp with confidence.

"Hold him steady," the guard said. Scorpius and his master leaned into the noble, pressing firmly as the guard made the first slice to enlarge the wound.

All Scorpius could think about were the men who had once held his master when he'd been put to the question. At least Lord Thibault's writhing and muffled shrieks were to heal a wound and not create one.

Yet wasn't the torment the same, whether it was inflicted with notorious brutality deep below the estate's splendor, or whether it happened here in their cozy falconer's cottage?

52

The detachment of guards thundered around the bend, their horses just as fierce-looking as the men who dismounted to spread quickly across the clearing. The bound courtiers were made to regret their choices of loyalties, even with their trial some days away.

Richolf motioned for Scorpius to stick close as the commanding officer strode across the cottage's stone floor. Scorpius' gut twisted with dread for Lord Thibault, who lay on their table still drenched in sweat from his ordeal.

The commander poked and prodded the noble, who answered in moans. "Looks clean," the officer said. "No poison."

He carried himself like a prince, or at least what Scorpius imagined a prince might look like. If he ignored the scars and the uniform, Scorpius would have wondered if this wasn't another royal sibling concealing his true rank as Lord Nizhnii had done years ago, before his brother's supporters had murdered him in the very dust outside the cottage.

"Just the arrow, sir," the guard who'd removed it said.

"Was there anyone with Lord Thibault when he was attacked?"

Scorpius' heart stopped in mid-beat. Richolf stepped ever so slightly ahead of him.

Gesturing towards Scorpius, the guard said, "The falconer's boy, sir."

The officer glanced across the kitchen to hold Scorpius in his piercing gaze. Everything inside of Scorpius shriveled to nothing.

At first he took a step back as the officer walked towards him. Forcing himself to stand straight, he recalled that he had, in fact, saved the young lord's life. The sight of Richolf's bowed head from the corner of his eye reminded Scorpius to do likewise, just in time.

"How did it happen?" the officer said.

Glancing up at Lord Thibault's sprawled form and bloodied shoulder, Scorpius took a deep breath and explained how the hunting party had turned on itself, describing his flight with the noble into the forest and their concealment beneath the rock ledge. At the end, he dared to look up into the commander's eyes.

The officer stepped even closer, nose to nose. Scorpius was forced to look down or be insubordinate.

For a long moment, the officer didn't speak. He merely stood there, too close, his gaze raking Scorpius from top to bottom, delving beneath his skin like a cruel knife looking for arrowheads or poison.

Swallowing hard, Scorpius stood as still as he could, his mouth dry, his palms sweaty.

"How did you know to run?" the officer asked, finally.

With every part of his being, Scorpius wanted to leave his master out of this, just in case there might be more questions to make Richolf suffer. Eventually Lord Thibault would tell his own version of the event, and the falconer was the one who'd alerted them to the danger. So that is what Scorpius told him.

Turning towards his master, the commander fired off a series of questions meant to trip up liars. Richolf answered everything calmly and simply, with the right amount of deference and the dignity of having nothing to hide.

The officer signaled for the guard to follow him outside. Without another word, they were gone.

Scorpius and Richolf exchanged pale glances. Yet they were not as pale as the young lord, who at least moaned to reassure them he lived.

53

Scorpius stood in the kitchen with his master, watching carefully as the apothecary's apprentice grated the fruit zest finely into the mortar. Raising one unimpressed eyebrow as he glanced up, checking to be sure they followed his instruction, the young man grabbed a pinch of forest herb from an open pouch on the counter, added a long list of ingredients and finally began crushing them all with the pestle.

Of course there was a particular technique that was vital to the success of the mixture. It was hard to take these edicts seriously, as there were so many of them, and so detailed. Scorpius noted that Richolf paid very close attention and did not shoot him any sideways glances.

So Scorpius forced himself to do likewise as the occasional moan drifted up from Lord Thibault, who rested in Richolf's shuttered room. The wound was deep and now festered, poison or no poison.

The young noble was too weak to be moved from the falconer's cottage. It was up to his master and himself to nurse the noble back to health. Lord Thibault's family could not afford to have their enemies track the comings and goings of healers to the falconer's cottage. One visit of this apothecary's apprentice was all that could be risked without arousing suspicion.

Granted, two of Lord Thibault's guard remained behind until their master could recover himself. They were stashed out of sight but within earshot, in the closest falcon mews behind the cottage.

His master had no need to tell Scorpius that the guard stationed behind to protect Lord Thibault was also meant to tidy up any loose ends if he succumbed to his wounds. No matter how revolting the apothecary apprentice's thick yellow paste looked and smelled, Scorpius memorized all of the ingredients used by the insufferable young man, his exacting methods in preparing them and in applying them.

For four days, his master cared for Lord Thibault. On the

fifth day, a small group of nobles arrived at the cottage for a hunt.

Richolf took them onto the field while Scorpius sat with Lord Thibault, a damp cloth for the noble's forehead in one hand, a concealed knife in the other.

And right outside the cottage window, he heard the stealthy approach of one of the guard, who stationed himself along the cottage's stone wall. Scorpius looked down at the knife in his clammy hand.

What could he do against one of the hardened men who had disarmed Lord Thibault's would-be assassins? And what about his master, alone with a hunting party who could be slitting the falconer's throat instead of watching the hawks take down their dinner?

54

Lord Thibault squirmed restlessly on the falconer's bed, soft sounds of distress escaping into the little room. Tiny bumps erupted over Scorpius' skin as he tried to sense the position of the guard outside, poised beneath the window.

The young noble's face lined with pain, his body stiffening as he coughed. Then for the first time in a day and a night, his eyes opened.

Scorpius' heart swelled with relief, though his fingers gripped the concealed knife handle even tighter.

Gaze roaming the unfamiliar room, Lord Thibault at last settled upon Scorpius' face. Tension fell away as he smiled a wan smile.

Scorpius leaned forward, placing a hand on the noble's hot brow, watching Lord Thibault's lips working to form Scorpius' name.

The noble's thready voice became an urgent whisper.

It was a female's voice — "Scorpius!"

Cocking his head, certain he must be hearing things, Scorpius caught a glimpse from the corner of his eye. Shiny hair smoothed back into a complex design followed by a finely-woven cloak rose up over the window ledge.

Scorpius surged forward to grasp the shoulders of the woman who slid down into the room. Kneeling to follow her descent, breaking her fall as well as he was able, Scorpius grunted as she turned with speed and force, pinning him to the ground.

Her fingers pressed hard against his lips.

Scorpius looked up into her eyes — and lay still.

It was Ingerith.

She saw his realization and relaxed her grip on his mouth. Scorpius' chest seized with emotion as she held a single finger before her lips. She waited until he nodded before climbing off of him.

Lord Thibault, too weak to defend himself, pushed upright

in the bed as far as he was able, holding his gaze steady if this was to be his last breath.

Thrusting a hand out to grab Ingerith's skirts, Scorpius held up his other hand to stop her. Scrambling to his knees, he sought Lord Thibault's gaze.

Then he looked up at his master's lover, who had helped Scorpius to mend Richolf's broken body after he'd been put to the question. Taking her hand in his, gazing over at Lord Thibault to be sure he watched, Scorpius bowed his head before her hand and then kissed it.

Ingerith looked down at him, her face flushed with emotion. The gaze they shared could only reach between two people who have made terrible memories together. Swallowing hard against them, Scorpius took her hand and moved it towards the bed, gesturing towards Lord Thibault with the other.

Nodding deeply twice, Scorpius saw the young noble's recognition of their offer. Lord Thibault relaxed and slid back along the pillow, again coughing painfully.

Crawling as quietly as he could, Scorpius grabbed up the ointment prepared by the apothecary's assistant and offered it to Ingerith. She brought it to her nose to discern its contents, dipped a finger in and rubbed the mixture between her fingers to get a feel for it.

Then she jerked her head forward to call for his assistance. Working together in silent swiftness, Ingerith and Scorpius peeled back the previous dressings on Lord Thibault's wound.

When it was treated, and before they let him collapse, Ingerith slipped a glass vial from her pocket, uncorked the lid, and tipped a mouthful into the young noble's mouth.

He downed it without any complaint other than a sour face. Ingerith turned to Scorpius and made gestures to indicate different positions of the sun in the sky, then counted out how many doses Lord Thibault must take.

Scorpius accepted the vial with a bowed head. She had once crossly forbid him to call her a lady, but these gestures of respect were the only ways he could think of to signal his understanding.

His heart leapt wildly when she pulled him close to her chest and placed a long kiss on the back of his head. Her skirts rustled, and when he looked up she was already being pulled back up through the window by the guard still waiting outside.

In a heartbeat she was gone, the only indication she'd ever been here being the glass vial in Scorpius' hand, and the tinge of color finally returning to Lord Thibault's cheeks.

55

His master's tiny room grew stale with Lord Thibault's fever sweat. The young noble shoved away the blanket or clutched it close in a rumpled knot, worrying Scorpius that the dressing would loosen.

Keeping to their normal schedule, Richolf saw to the falcons, took hunting parties out onto the field and prepared meals until Scorpius longed for nothing more than to have his old chores returned to him. Yet his master saw how Lord Thibault responded to Scorpius.

"He trusts you," Richolf said in a low voice as Scorpius joined him for a brief supper at the table. "He'll heal more quickly if he's not on guard."

Scorpius nodded wearily, wishing he could have even an hour to walk out into the forest. When he gazed up at his master, he saw the deep lines in Richolf's face, the shadows beneath his eyes, the hunched curve of his shoulders.

"Would you not care to sit with him awhile, sir? It will do you some good. I can see to the rest of the work before turning in."

A rueful smile tilted his master's lips. "Best for you to stay with him."

Scorpius nodded, looking down at his plate of food, the weight of his responsibility to restore the young noble to health making it hard to take a breath. It wasn't long before he sat on the stool beside the bed, coaxing Lord Thibault to take sips of broth from a worn mug.

The young noble trembled with the effort to sit upright. His color remained pale, his hair damp and plastered to his forehead. Had there been any complaints from this noble? Not even after they dug the arrow from his shoulder. He'd suffered through it all without a cross word.

Looking away in shame, Scorpius thought of the healing salve he'd need to mix up later this evening. He didn't see the noble reach for him, and was startled by the touch of Lord

Thibault's hand on his own.

He dropped the mug into the noble's lap, warm broth soaking into Lord Thibault's trousers.

For a long moment, neither of them moved.

Then, as though freed from a spell, Scorpius jumped to his feet, whisking away the mug and grabbing the blanket to sop up the mess.

"I suppose that's one way to make sure I get a bath," Lord Thibault said.

"You needed one long before this," Scorpius said, dumping the blanket in a sodden heap in the corner. The words were already out of his mouth before he realized how annoyed he sounded, how little like a falconer's apprentice addressing a lord.

He stopped what he was doing and turned to Lord Thibault, bowing his head low. "Forgive me, my lord."

The silence stretched in the stuffy little room. Scorpius' skin prickled as he waited, until at last the young noble said, "Come."

Risking a glance up, Scorpius saw that Lord Thibault had moved as far from the damp spot as he could manage on his own. That effort had broken him into a new sweat. Scorpius strode forward and knelt close to the side of the bed.

Once again, the young noble reached his hand out and covered Scorpius' with his own. Scorpius looked down at Lord Thibault's fingers squeezing his with the promise of renewed strength.

"I was trying to thank you," Lord Thibault said.

Scorpius shook his head, still not looking up. "No need, my lord."

"Well, you don't make it easy, I'll say that."

Gazing up then, Scorpius looked into Lord Thibault's eyes. They twinkled with unspoken laughter. The young noble squeezed his hand again and let go, his body suddenly racked with coughing.

Passing him the only kerchief left — the one tucked in his own doublet — Scorpius watched as Lord Thibault checked the color of his spit. No blood.

The young noble looked at Scorpius with relief and gratitude so raw it made Scorpius uneasy. How hard it must be never to feel free to trust anyone. He thought of how much he'd longed to leave Richolf to all of this nursing, but his master had known how it was for Lord Thibault.

"Shall I fetch you more broth, my lord?"

"As long as I may finish it this time."

"The thing to remember is to get it into your mouth, my lord."

Lord Thibault's eyes widened, his lips opening to speak — but nothing came out. Scorpius couldn't hold back a smile before he ducked out of the room for the kitchen.

56

Lord Thibault's weight dragged upon Scorpius' shoulders, and upon his master's, also. Every movement sounded so very loud in the stillness of night, but they kept onward all the same.

They could not afford a light, but Richolf's years in these woods made their path clear. Stopping every so often so the noble could rest, they picked their way past branches and over stumps until Scorpius heard Lord Thibault's mount jingling his tack in the darkness.

A wash of relief spread through Scorpius' chest once they'd hoisted the noble into the saddle. He tried to look at Richolf through the gloom, but only his form stood out from the night woods.

"Scorpius," Lord Thibault whispered.

He moved close to the horse, standing beside the noble's boot snug in the stirrup. Realizing Lord Thibault was tapping the saddlebag, Scorpius' fingers slid along the leather until he found the buckle. Unfastening it as quietly as he could, he reached into the deep pouch until his hand bumped against a cloth sack. He pulled its heavy weight up out of the saddlebag and moved to hand it to Lord Thibault.

The young noble wrapped his hands around Scorpius'. Looking up to see Lord Thibault's silhouette against the trees, Scorpius heard the command to pass the sack of coins over to Richolf. His heart pounded with frightening insistence.

Dizzy with dread that pierced him like the killing talons of their falcons, Scorpius stumbled forward until Richolf stepped in front of him. His master's familiar, weathered hands covered Scorpius', helping him to withstand the burden of the coins for a long moment.

Tears burned down Scorpius' face as Richolf took the sack and set it on the ground. Grabbing Scorpius by the arm to steady him, Richolf turned and Scorpius followed until they both stood beside Lord Thibault astride his stallion.

"My family is grateful for your service, falconer," the noble said in a voice still weak with pain.

Richolf bowed even though it was so dark. "My lord."

"We would not see you suffer on my behalf. Those who would have killed me here will send others to make you pay for their failure."

Richolf took a deep breath, then said, his voice breaking, "I understand, my lord."

Scorpius felt sick. He could hardly get his breath.

"He will come with me," Lord Thibault said, as if Scorpius was not right there. "I cannot afford to lose him."

It took a moment for Richolf to force the words out. "As you will, my lord."

"Master," Scorpius whispered. If only he could see Richolf's face.

Strong arms wrapped around him. Scorpius grabbed hold of Richolf as if his embrace could stop this from happening.

"Take care, Scorpius," Richolf said, stepping back, still holding him by the arms. "Promise me."

"Where will you go?" Scorpius said, his voice thick with the sobs that were far too dangerous for this night.

His master grabbed hold of his face and kissed him hard on the forehead. "I will send word when I can. When it is safe enough."

Scorpius trembled. This couldn't be happening.

Richolf released him, bent to scoop up the sack of coins and disappeared into the black arms of the forest.

Gazing over to see the patient form of Lord Thibault upon his horse, Scorpius fought the urge to knock the young noble to the ground, wishing with all of his might that this lord had never ridden around the curve of the road that led to the home Scorpius had shared with Richolf for a decade.

It wasn't too late. He could run after Richolf. The two of them could find another place for themselves, a place far away from all of the murderous games these nobles played, not caring whom they eliminated along the way.

He listened closely, but the forest was still. No sign of his master, nor which direction he'd taken.

There was only Lord Thibault. Scorpius still recalled the weight of him as he'd dragged the young noble to safety beneath the rock ledge and the roots of the ancient tree. The hair on the back of Scorpius' neck prickled as he remembered the shrieks Lord Thibault had made as the arrowhead was dug out of his shoulder. Scorpius flexed his fingers, almost feeling the knife handle he'd gripped, ready to use it when Ingerith slid through the window with a healing draught for this young noble.

Swiping the tears away, Scorpius strode forward, taking his new master's outstretched hand to haul himself up onto the horse. With silent signals between stallion and rider, Lord Thibault turned them away from the falconer's wood, plunging deeper into the forest.

57

Pulling the reins taut, Lord Thibault stopped them at the edge of a hill overlooking a fortified estate. The approaching dawn revealed laborers already wading out into the fields, watched by overseers.

"I should have asked you this before," the young noble said, his voice barely audible from weariness and caution.

Scorpius recoiled a little from Lord Thibault, releasing his hold upon him from his perch in the saddle. The sight of the masters keeping watchful eye over those serving in the field brought it all back to him — the screams that hung in the air of the Nightmare Hunt.

"There is something I must ask of you. Something very hard," Lord Thibault said.

Scorpius' lungs tightened with dread. Recalling the weight of the coins this noble had delivered to Richolf, urging him to embrace life when it was in danger, Scorpius took a deep breath and said, "Then ask it, my lord."

The noble bowed his head for a long moment. Then he twisted back to gaze at Scorpius as far as his shoulder wound allowed. "This is my uncle's estate. If we stop here before returning home, we can set events in motion that will see justice delivered for your master."

"My lord?" The desire for revenge flared inside Scorpius' chest. How swiftly it took flight, yet he hadn't realized it even lived inside of him.

"This will take some days to reach fruition. Days you will find very hard."

"Why should you care about my master, my lord? What is he to you?"

"It is not what he means to me, but what he means to you that concerns me. You will need to hold onto that dearly."

Scorpius said nothing, so Lord Thibault continued.

"During my first visit to the falconry, I noticed a scar upon your master's neck. It had a singular shape which I recognized."

Scorpius knew it well. Only Ingerith's intervention had healed such a vile piece of torn flesh.

"When I was a boy," Lord Thibault said, "I was taken to the deepest corner of my uncle's holdings. It was meant to toughen me, for one day I would be asked to put men to such torments in my turn.

"There was a demonstration of the question being put to an unfortunate fellow, and a grievous wound made that held the shape of the falconer's scar. The man wielding the iron took special pride in fashioning his own tools. So I know who it was that tormented your master. And this knowledge gives me the missing proof for my own justice, proof I've sought out for most of my life."

Perhaps Scorpius should have felt his blood chilling with fear at the thought that Lord Thibault had played a flawless hand. The young noble's continued dismissal of Richolf in favor of Scorpius had pulled the veil over any hint of interest in the falconer and his telltale scar.

Instead, the memory of the coin bag's weight as he passed it to his master fanned the embers burning in his heart. This noble could have sent Richolf into the darkness with nothing.

"What would you have me do, my lord?"

"It will be hard."

"How long have you waited to find the scar upon my master?"

Lord Thibault looked across the fields at the estate. "Whatever you think 'hard' will be, the 'hard' I'm warning you about is far worse."

"And yet you ask it of me."

Birdsong filled the silence between them.

"My father knew that one day I would be called upon to send men to their deaths," Lord Thibault said. "Or worse. To wish for death and not be granted that release. He schooled me to rule, and I did not shy away from his lessons.

"Yes, I am asking you to do this, Scorpius. A request. Not a command.

"I'm going to ride into my uncle's courtyard, and if you're still on the back of this horse I will present you as my prisoner. You will be the one who took me from the falconer's field and held me on behalf of your master.

"They will not believe your master was the falconer if I've taken the trouble to capture you. Fortunately for my purposes, you will not be able to answer any of their questions. This will make my version of what happened ring true."

The burning rush through Scorpius' veins gave way to icy fear. Lord Thibault was young, but he continued to play his hand with the sureness of a red-tail swooping low over the field.

"I will do as you ask, my lord," he said, his voice trembling.

58

Scorpius stared at the pebbles at his feet, the same pebbles at which he'd been staring since dawn first broke and Lord Thibault had delivered him to his uncle in the guise of a prisoner.

How much longer would he be forced to linger here, arms wrenched behind him, chained high upon the stone column, forcing Scorpius to bend forward to stare at the pebbles? His back had gone through a rising wave of agony throughout the day, but he found that if he could remain as still as possible, the pain held its breath.

He needed to shift position.

Yet another biting fly made up his mind for him. It landed on his cheek in the rivulet of sweat and blood left from the guard's blow. Shaking his head to dislodge the fly, Scorpius sent a forked bolt of agony through his hips, up his spine, flaring out across his shoulders, snaking up his arms and exploding along his neck into his head.

Gasping with the force of it, Scorpius squeezed his eyes tight, tears joining the sweat, the blood, the dirt, and the matted hair that stuck to his face.

It will be hard, his new master had said. He'd known what Scorpius would face.

Taking as deep a breath as he dared, Scorpius concentrated on the memory of Lord Thibault writhing upon the table as the guard had dug the arrowhead from his shoulder. He remembered just how it had felt to press with all of his might against the young noble's attempts to get away from the pain.

His new master was now laying the framework to wrestle justice from his would-be assassins. Scorpius no longer served a falconer — he served a young noble whose life would always be in danger. So here Scorpius hung in chains in the relentless sun.

His stomach rumbled as he thought of the young noble sitting down to eat. Stretching out his tongue, Scorpius licked the sweat from his upper lip. He had not eaten in a very long time.

In fact, no one had come to check on him in hours. He was

bound here in a walled-in courtyard quite apart from everything and everyone. He could hear sounds of life just over the wall, but here there were just the pebbles, the sweat, the flies, the pain and his own desire for revenge.

If he put his faith in his new master who had his own score to settle, the torments once visited upon his former master Richolf would come full circle upon whomever had been responsible for them. Until the gray hours of this morning, Scorpius hadn't even hoped such a thing could come to pass.

So he hung here, the iron cutting into his wrists, his head swirling with fatigue, his muscles seizing up to draw cries from his cracked lips.

When he finally heard the creak of a door and the rhythmic cadence of footsteps, the jingling of keys and the solid sway of a guard's uniform, Scorpius didn't know whether he should be grateful or terrified. It didn't take long before he knew it was the latter.

The guard released the shackles from the rings embedded in the stone column, only to grab hold of Scorpius' aching arms, shoving him forward still bound. Scorpius stumbled on legs that were stiff and swollen. Slaps from the guard spurred him forward.

He entered a cool corridor, so dark after the day he'd spent in the sun that he was as good as blind. He trembled as the sweat chilled on his skin, fear stealing his breath. Kicks from the guard kept him moving.

The corridor turned, revealing a door. A young guard stood at the ready beside it, nodding at Scorpius' escort and pushing the door open.

The room was empty except for a stool, a rough table and a chair, upon which sat an imposing man in noble attire. Another man turned to fix Scorpius with a stare that shriveled any semblance of courage that had ever existed inside him.

The guard shoved him forward. Scorpius landed on his face at the lord's feet.

59

Rising stiffly to his knees, arms still wrenched behind him by the iron shackles, Scorpius glanced up into the eyes of the noble.

He was a heartbeat away from lowering his gaze. Serving such men at the hunt demanded it.

He saw clearly in his mind how the courtiers had sat there glaring, even chained to the hitching posts, even with bruises and swollen lips. The guard detachment had dealt them a bitter taste as to what they could expect, once it came time to answer for their assassination attempt upon his new master. Yet it had not altered their demeanor in the slightest. They'd not hung their heads nor cowered nor looked away.

So Scorpius wrestled down Richolf's training to return the nobleman's stare as though he had a right to do it. After all, hadn't his former master fetched him from the nursery? Scorpius had been raised to be a little lord himself until the falconer had arrived, providing him with the sanctuary of life out at their cottage.

"Name," the guard said.

Maintaining eye contact with the noble, as if it were beneath him to address a guard, he said, "Scorpius."

"Your master," the guard continued.

Scorpius turned his gaze toward him this time — and his breath hitched in his chest. It was the captain who'd ridden around the bend towards the cottage with the detachment after the guard's successful removal of the arrowhead from Lord Thibault's shoulder. He'd seen Scorpius at the falconer's cottage with his own eyes.

Blinking rapidly, Scorpius forced himself to trust in what his new master said: *They will not believe your master was the falconer*. If that were the case, the guard captain could think as he liked. He looked away from the captain who'd carried himself like a prince that day, once again addressing only the noble. "I have none," he said as dismissively as he could.

"All men have masters," the lord said, his deep silky voice suited to a castle's great hall and not this dank cell. His mouth turned up in a wry smile. "Even I have masters."

The captain moved slowly to circle behind Scorpius. "You're a mercenary, then."

"No." He'd almost said *No, sir.* "No, no mercenary."

Yanking Scorpius' head back hard, the captain said, "How much did they pay you?"

Turning his alarm into outrage, Scorpius stared down the noble and said nothing. These men no doubt assumed that eventually they would get what they wanted from him. Whether they believed he was a noble or a servant, it was held to be a truth that every man had his breaking point.

Yet Scorpius' former master had been put to the question and had never broken.

True, his body held the scars that had given Lord Thibault the ammunition he'd needed for his current attempt to right an old wrong. It was also true that Richolf still woke in the night, shrieking and sweating, even all these years later.

Richolf had survived their torments without giving up the information for which they'd pressed. Perhaps that was why Scorpius was able to meet the quizzical stare of the noble, even as the captain's fingers pulled cruelly at his hair.

He knew it was possible to survive whatever these men had planned for him. He knew it, and they did not. Yes, he trembled — who would not, after the day he'd spent in chains? Yes, his stomach flipped with dread — if he did not fear what lay in store for him, having treated his former master's wounds himself, he would not be in control of his senses.

"Come, come," the noble said suddenly, addressing the captain and flicking his head toward the stool. "Let us not distress our guest."

Hoisting Scorpius to his feet, the captain dragged him forward to sit roughly upon the stool. How he wished the captain would not stand behind him like that.

The noble rose from his chair to approach Scorpius. Taking deep breaths, Scorpius fought to ignore the way his heart hammered so loudly. In the few short steps it would take to reach him, the lord meant to unravel what his former master had suffered so much to give him.

Clenching his bound fists behind him, Scorpius held his head high, staring hard at the wall in the distance. Whatever they meant to ask him, he did not know the answers. It was just a matter of endurance.

Why should you care about my master, my lord? he'd asked Lord Thibault, when they'd still sat upon his horse in safety, on the edge of the estate. *What is he to you?*

"It is not what he means to me," his new master had cautioned, "but what he means to you that concerns me. You will need to hold onto that dearly."

In the damp echoing cell, Scorpius filled his mind with the memory of Richolf and held onto it. Richolf had endured. He would show Scorpius how to do the same.

60

"You have no master, you say," the noble said. His deep, silky voice caressed Scorpius' neck, his lips nearly grazing his ear.

Clenching his bound hands behind him, Scorpius fought the urge to cringe away from the lord. It wasn't easy. Lightheaded with his heart beating so fast, he feared pitching backwards off the stool. "None," he said, his voice betraying his fear.

The guard captain closed in behind him, leaning forward to speak over his head to the noble. "No master to look for him should he not return."

Straightening, the noble said, "Yet he must have family awaiting him."

Scorpius' mouth went dry. He stared hard across the cell, his mind flashing back to his young days in the nursery, waiting to be visited by his parents as all the other boys and girls were visited. He remembered vividly the sight of Richolf with his grim, scarred face, speaking to Nurse, then turning to claim him.

"No master," Scorpius said, his voice weary with the truth of it. "No family."

The noble exchanged glances with the captain. "Conjured out of thin air, were you?"

The mention of magicke — the spectre of being accused of any knowledge of it — seized Scorpius with an alarming urge to puke. The threat of being burnt alive filled the cell like a lightning bolt. "Begotten as you were begotten," Scorpius said, shocked that any words had formed at all.

An explosion of pain nearly wrenched his head from his shoulders. Toppling from the stool, he sprawled upon the stone floor, his bound hands unable to stop his fall.

"I doubt his lordship entered this world as you did," the captain said.

Shaking his head to clear it, Scorpius said, "As *you* were begotten, then."

The captain lunged to strike him again, but a mere tap from the noble stopped him in his tracks. No blows, only assistance to sit once more upon the stool.

"Lord Thibault's father will not be as welcoming as I," the noble said, pacing slowly.

Shivering at the idea of lesser generosity, Scorpius held his tongue and tried to keep track of the captain's whereabouts from the corner of his eye.

"Although no doubt he will reward those who came to his son's assistance," the captain said from very close behind him. Scorpius jerked away from his voice as though singed.

"No matter," the lord said. "This one will soon be wearing his reward."

Circling in front of him, the guard captain roughly loosened Scorpius' jerkin and tunic. Scorpius' pulse hammered in his veins as the captain took several steps to stand behind him once more.

Gathering every strand of courage blowing loosely inside of him, Scorpius sought the gaze of the noble as rough fingers yanked his clothing down to his waist, as far as the iron shackles would allow. He watched as the expression quickly changed on the lord's face, confidence giving way to dread.

"No marks, my lord," the captain said.

Scorpius thought of the young guard flogged to a bloody mess during the Nightmare Hunt. Shaken by the force of gratitude for his unscarred back, Scorpius tried to cover his emotion by thrusting his chin forward, again seeking the gaze of the noble. Stepping close, the lord pulled up Scorpius' tunic and jerkin himself.

"As I said, let's not distress our guest," the noble said, as though Scorpius wasn't trapped in this cell with his arms bound and bruises forming.

"We'll leave that to the duke," said the guard captain, and the two men chuckled.

61

"How did my nephew come to overpower such a foe?" the noble asked, as though Lord Thibault wouldn't be capable of such a thing under normal circumstances.

The smooth back which Richolf had safeguarded for him made Scorpius appear to be one of the blood. His former master could have wielded cruel lessons during his apprenticeship, but had never done so.

"You think he could best me in a fight?" Scorpius said with disdain.

"No. I am certain he could not," the noble said.

Scorpius tried to ignore the flutter of pride that rose inside of him at those words.

"He made you his prisoner somehow," the guard captain said.

Once again ignoring the captain as though it were beneath Scorpius to address him, he said, "Does it matter how he put me here? I shall be delivered to the duke soon enough."

Both men laughed a second time, a chilling sound that raised the bumps on Scorpius' skin. "A distressing prospect, to be certain," the noble said.

Scorpius thought of his new master, how they had laughed together, suffered together. He thought of how generous Lord Thibault had been to Richolf, who meant more to Scorpius than anyone in the world. How could Lord Thibault's father carry a reputation that filled men with such dread?

"Other men would be trying to forge a deal about now, would they not, my lord?" the captain said.

"Men with families and masters, you mean?" Scorpius said, looking off into the shadows.

"Perhaps I could offer you one or the other." The noble leaned forward and took Scorpius' chin in one hand.

Scorpius did not meet his gaze. He tried to free himself from the lord's grasp, but it only made the noble squeeze painfully.

"Perhaps it's time for you to stop roaming. Start giving

allegiance to one house. One family."

Wishing the lord's words didn't cut so close to the bone, Scorpius asked, "Why should you want me?" He was surprised to see an answering desperation in the noble's eyes.

"The winds of discontent blow across this dominion. And yet only the first droplets of blood have been shed. It's not every day an unclaimed man of your stature arrives at my door. I offer position, weapons and an income."

Scorpius noticed the captain had circled around so that both men stared at him. The captain's gaze roamed as though already fitting Scorpius out with a uniform and a blade.

"If you agree, I could send my nephew home without you. There would be no reason to discuss anything at all with the duke."

What was going on? Scorpius suddenly felt like a game hen thrown down before the hunting dogs. "I shall take my chances," he said, looking away.

The lord and the captain looked at one another in disbelief.

"I'm offering you an opportunity to stay here in one piece," the noble said.

"Yes, and of course that is very kind of you," Scorpius said.

The captain darted forward, once again grabbing Scorpius by a handful of hair. Forced to stare into the guard's face, Scorpius got the eerie sensation that this man was somehow looking through him.

"You're hiding something," the captain said.

"You can ask the duke what it was when he's done with me," Scorpius said.

The guard released him and stepped back, just as the noble took a few steps forward. "If you share this information with me rather than with the duke, I could arrange for you to have more than a position. I could arrange a title for you."

Scorpius heart seized up inside his chest. What kind of torment was this? Offering his every heart's desire instead of slicking the stone floor with his blood? What sort of information did they think he possessed?

It was madness. He felt dizzy and nauseous.

The terrible images of his childhood rushed forward just then, filled with lords stabbing one another on the falconer's doorstep, with a pale body dragged off for the dragon to destroy the evidence.

Perhaps he did know something after all. He looked across the cell at the noble and the guard captain. Just as he'd sensed in the market square when he'd bartered for Richolf's pelts, he felt the tide turn here in this clammy cell.

The shackles still dug into his wrists, his shoulders and legs still ached from his day of forced standing. He was in a stone cell beneath the noble's estate. Yet quite suddenly he felt as though he sat high upon Lord Thibault's stallion.

Strange, how his mind worked so hard to break him out of this gloom. In this landscape, his mind was his most important weapon. A stout heart could languish here for months. A sharp mind could defend him when his height and strength were bound and useless.

Scorpius looked away from his tormentors, dismissing them as he had been dismissed so many times after the hunt. He felt the ripple of their frustration in the close confines of the cell. A smile wanted to tug at his lips, but he knew he could not pull off something so daring. It was enough to feel the smile lighting his courage.

62

Scorpius woke from a fitful haze as the cell door creaked open. Rising stiffly to his knees, he saw his master's uncle and the captain of the guard enter, each one stepping aside as Lord Thibault strode forward to regard him.

Scorpius fought hard to erase any hint of the relief he felt at his new master's return. Perhaps Lord Thibault meant to make it easier for him... when he suddenly planted his foot on Scorpius' chest and shoved, slamming him onto the stone floor. If he hadn't met his new master before now, Lord Thibault's expression would have scattered his courage into the darkest corners of this cell.

"He looks well enough," the young noble said. "Have him brought to my horse. I am bound for home."

The captain bowed in a sweeping gesture, departing the cell with a backward glance at Scorpius. It made the hair on his body stand on end.

Once again, he recalled the pitying laughter from Lord Thibault's uncle and the captain at their threat of turning him over to the duke. As far as they were concerned, the threat had just become Scorpius' fate.

He must remember to play his role.

Glancing up at the uncle, he begged silently to be allowed to stay and serve him, as the noble had offered but Scorpius had refused. The older man caught his meaning and glanced quickly at the open cell door, waiting for the captain's return.

Lord Thibault shoved hard at Scorpius with his foot before removing it. "My father will be pleased to make your acquaintance."

Scrambling to his knees, Scorpius bowed low and let the chilly damp set him to shivering.

"The poor fellow seems put off by your father, the duke," said the uncle.

"It is not his intelligence I question, but his loyalties." Lord Thibault sat upon the table, and Scorpius saw that his master had weakened himself with that display of aggression.

"Tricky, that," his uncle said. "Your father expects you, then?"

"I doubt it. I made my way to you as soon as I made a prisoner of my captor."

"Yes, I admit I was so very curious about that," the noble said. "He seems a hard one to best."

Once again, Scorpius' chest flushed with pride at the uncle's assessment of his strength and skill. Though it was laughable to think that an unschooled falconer's apprentice could overpower the highly-trained son of a duke.

"Seems a waste to let your father break such a man," said the uncle.

Scorpius' blood chilled. His new master's father filled him with foreboding. His heartbeat quickened as he heard several footsteps making their rhythmic way along the corridor. Looking up as if in a panic towards the uncle, Scorpius saw the man pale slightly.

"Is there no way to take him off your hands?" the noble said. Gazing down into Scorpius' eyes, the uncle's pity reached across the cell, touching Scorpius so that his heart swelled with an irrational hope.

"I understand your feelings, uncle. I do. Must we not see justice done?"

"Of course, you're right," the uncle said as the captain returned with another very large guard carrying a long rope.

"On your feet," the captain barked, and in a blur Scorpius was hauled upright, his hands tugged forward by the brutish new guard and secured before him. Dragged forward, Scorpius stumbled until the corridor lightened and he was pushed from behind into the sunlight.

His new master took his leave from his uncle as the guard captain secured the long rope to the back of Lord Thibault's saddle. Staring in dismay at the uncle, Scorpius' stomach twisted when the older man couldn't return his gaze.

Clucking at the horse, Lord Thibault set him to a walk,

which propelled Scorpius forward, arms yanked so that his sore shoulders flared with new protests. Ignoring the stares and taunts of the people as they passed, Scorpius kept his gaze on the road before him. He dare not trip, for his new master would be obliged to drag him for a pace until he regained his feet.

63

Lord Thibault slid down from the saddle, unsteady on his feet. Scorpius rushed forward to offer assistance, but his master barked at him to stay put.

He turned away, increasing the pull on his bound wrists, before Lord Thibault could see the outrage flaring inside of him.

"Take your rest," his master ordered, fumbling at the saddlebags.

When Scorpius failed to move, Lord Thibault said, "Now!"

A painful weight wrapped around Scorpius' heart. He sat on the side of the road, looking back the way they'd come, unwilling to entertain the thoughts that had been swirling inside of him for miles now. Staring at the rope that tied him to his master's horse, he recalled the dark laughter of Lord Thibault's uncle and the guard captain whenever they mentioned his master's father.

The closer they'd come to the duke's residence, the more remote Lord Thibault had become. Scorpius tested his bonds, but he'd been tied securely. He was weakened from forced standing in the sun, from not enough food or water, from the cold dampness of the cell where they'd bloodied and bruised him.

There must be a reason for such dread shown towards his master's father. Though they'd been on the road for a good hour, still Lord Thibault paraded him as a captive, even here in this forest clearing under the watchful eyes of only birds and forest creatures.

He clearly remembered the look in his new master's eyes when he'd come to collect him from his uncle. Lord Thibault had shown a chilling side that Scorpius had never suspected could lurk inside the young noble whose life he'd saved, whom he'd nursed back to health, and who had sent his former master on his way, not with a command but with a sack of coin.

As Lord Thibault's footsteps neared, Scorpius moved to his knees and bowed his head. If his new master was turning out to be his father's son, Scorpius had better start showing some proper deference. He didn't expect the pit that formed in his gut at having to carve out this sinister new relationship. Where was the young noble he'd once laughed with back at the forest pool in the falconer's wood?

His master lowered himself to one knee and offered a wineskin to Scorpius' lips. "Drink," he said.

"Thank you, my lord," Scorpius said, grateful for the dark liquid.

"I didn't take you for such an ass," Lord Thibault said in the barest of whispers.

Scorpius couldn't help it. He looked directly into his master's eyes as he drank.

He could have leaped and sung for joy. His true master stared back at him, even through the worry, fatigue and carefully-wrought persona.

Lord Thibault stood and took a long swig from the wineskin. Scorpius made sure to stare only at the road in front of him.

"We must go on this way, I'm afraid," his new master said as quietly as possible. "My enemies will have spies following our journey. They watch us even now."

Scorpius gazed out into the leafy shadows beyond the road. "How far, my lord?"

"We'll be another few hours on the road."

Taking a deep breath, Scorpius felt his aches rise up in protest. He said only, "You seem unwell, my lord."

His master remained silent for a long moment. "You ask me that, and me dragging you behind my horse?"

"Hardly dragging, my lord."

"You must enter my father's house a prisoner. Once behind closed doors, you shall be rewarded for your service to me, Scorpius. The spies will see what they were sent to see, but my father will welcome the man who restored his son."

Scorpius couldn't stop himself. "Please, my lord," he said, forcing himself to keep his gaze averted. "Why do men speak of your father, the duke, with such fear?"

"Because my father is a tyrant and a brute," Lord Thibault said, strolling back to the horse to climb into the saddle.

64

Scorpius followed Lord Thibault down the long gallery, their footsteps echoing against the polished wood. His master's cheeks flushed as they neared the double doors, which only served to make the pit in Scorpius' stomach grow heavier.

"Remember to address him as 'Your Grace,'" Lord Thibault said in a low voice.

"I'll remember, my lord."

The two servants flanking the doors turned to grasp the handles.

"I am not a favorite of his," Lord Thibault said, looking off into the distance.

The doors pushed open, to reveal a dark room that bristled with mounted weapons and hunting trophies. An imposing man turned from conversation to regard them as Lord Thibault stiffened, then forced himself to walk forward.

Scorpius' heart forgot to beat. Then it pounded so loudly he could barely think. His legs threatened to buckle, yet somehow he kept pace with his master and entered the duke's reception room. The doors shut solidly behind them.

The man speaking with the duke withdrew to a respectful distance as Lord Thibault approached his father. Scorpius halted, hoping he'd not already overstepped his place. The duke was too focused on his son, however, to notice anyone else.

Lord Thibault dropped to one knee, surging forward to grasp the duke's hand and kiss it. "Father," he whispered in a thick voice.

The duke's face softened for a fleeting moment. Then he bid his son to rise.

Scorpius used every shred of courage he possessed to remain standing as his master and his father, the duke turned to regard him. Gazing down at the impossibly ornate rug upon which he stood, Scorpius felt his skin prickle with the desire to be anywhere but here.

"And whom have you brought before me?" the duke said.

Lord Thibault swept his arm wide to invite Scorpius closer, which set off a great battle inside of him. *Move*, his brain commanded, but his limbs would not obey. Was he to kneel? Kiss the duke's hand?

His whole body trembled. His stomach rolled as if he might be sick.

Scorpius' master stood with arm outstretched, the duke looking on. He must not humiliate Lord Thibault before such a father, especially as he was not his favorite. Though it felt as though he lurched forward like a drunk, Scorpius strode towards the duke and bowed with deep grace, pulling his arm elegantly towards his heart.

"This is Scorpius, Your Grace," his master said. "He's the one who saved me from my murderers."

"Is he, now?"

Scorpius remained bowed, especially as the duke closed the distance between them.

"He looks a sight. Did you not think to refresh yourselves?"

When the duke turned, Scorpius shot a look over at Lord Thibault, who flicked his head to indicate that Scorpius could release his reverence. Taking his cue from the other man still in the room with them, Scorpius straightened, standing tall but with lowered gaze.

"You think to keep him, do you?" the duke said, his voice tight with derision.

"He has already served me as well as anyone has ever served our House."

The duke turned, grabbing his son and roughly yanking away his doublet and tunic from his shoulder. Lord Thibault's raw scars from the arrow brought the attempt on the young noble's life into the room with them.

"Could he not prevent this?" The duke released Lord Thibault to stumble and hurriedly recover himself.

"The only one who could have prevented it is the one who sent his assassins after me," Scorpius' master said.

With a dismissive grunt, the duke paced around Scorpius

before returning to the man whose conversation they'd interrupted. "Your mother awaits you," the duke said.

Lord Thibault bowed. "Your Grace," he said, already sweeping away to grab Scorpius by the arm and head for the double doors in long, bounding strides. The servants scrambled to open the doors in time.

"The fates have blessed us," Lord Thibault whispered, dashing along the corridor so that Scorpius had to scurry to keep up.

"My lord?" Scorpius asked.

"That was the chancellor in there with him. My father the duke was much distracted by whatever business they had together."

Scorpius thought of the rough way the duke had disrobed his son. "This went well, then?"

"*Very* well," Lord Thibault said, a wide grin lighting his face. Scorpius hadn't seen its like since the young noble had first rounded the corner of the falconer's cottage on his black stallion.

He followed his master through a maze of twists and turns until one of the corridors unfolded to reveal another set of double doors. This time, Lord Thibault was too quick for the young lads on either side of it. He yanked both doors wide open.

"Thibault! My darling boy!" a woman's voice called from within, until all was kisses and sobs of joy.

65

For a moment, Scorpius remained in the corridor with the two servants who flanked the doors. The emotion from within the dukessa's drawing room was too raw.

He tried to make eye contact with one of the lads. When he resolutely averted his gaze, Scorpius wondered at his role here. Was he not considered a servant? Lord Thibault's father, the duke had all but referred to him as a stray dog.

"Scorpius? Where have you got to...?" Lord Thibault rounded the door, face alight with joy.

"Come and meet my mother," he said, taking hold of Scorpius' shoulders to usher him forward into the dukessa's presence.

Scorpius' heart stuck in his chest at her shining beauty.

Lord Thibault's mother sat upon a lounging sofa in a cloud of silks, surrounded by two girls and a boy, the youngest of whom raced forward to grab Scorpius by the hand, dragging him forward. Every face shone with gratitude.

As soon as the young boy released him, Scorpius made the same reverence to Lord Thibault's mother as he'd made to the duke, bowing deeply, sweeping his arm to his heart.

"Mother, this is Scorpius. I would not be here standing before you, if it were not for him."

Scorpius heard the tremble of emotion in his master's voice. Stealing a glance at Lord Thibault, he saw the humbled gratitude which his master had dared not show his father. It made Scorpius' face flush hot.

"Come closer," the dukessa commanded. Scorpius' skin prickled as he straightened and approached her.

"Closer," she said, so he knelt before her. When she took hold of his face with delicate fingers and kissed the top of his head, Scorpius could not stop the gasp from escaping his lips.

Nearly bolting backwards, Scorpius regained his feet and took a step back, bowing his head.

The young boy wrapped his arm around Lord Thibault as the girls giggled at Scorpius. It was easier to glance at them than at the dukessa's radiance.

"He will be my new man," Lord Thibault said. Scorpius' heart warmed at the pride in his master's voice. It gave him the courage to look up, just as the dukessa's dark-eyed gaze came to rest upon him once more.

Scorpius couldn't shake the unsettling impression that this woman could somehow see through him, as though he were a veil. He saw understanding dawn in her eyes before he forced himself to look away.

"You must tell me everything," she said.

Glancing at the children present, Scorpius wondered for a moment whether he should spare the grimmest of the details. When he looked again at the dukessa, a part of him cautioned that she would somehow know whether he held anything back.

So he began at that moment when his former master, the falconer silently warned him from across the hunting field to run from the assassins. He watched as the boy's face paled when Scorpius described how he'd hauled the injured Lord Thibault to safety beneath the rock ledge. The girls reached for one another as he told of the terrible removal of the arrowhead from their brother's shoulder, while the dukessa wiped at her cheeks when he told of Ingerith's risky visit, bringing the tonic that cured Lord Thibault of the wound fever.

When he got to the part when Lord Thibault passed the sack of coins to his former master, parting so suddenly in the night woods, Scorpius' voice thickened and he couldn't go on.

Lord Thibault placed his hand upon Scorpius' shoulder. "He is a jewel among men, Mother."

"If it was an easy thing to unearth such treasures, my darling, they would hold no worth. Agridha, please fetch my trinket box."

The eldest girl crossed the room to retrieve a simple-looking wooden box from a drawer. Accepting it from her daughter, the dukessa opened the latch and lifted the lid.

Suddenly Scorpius realized that every eye was upon him.

A firm nudge from his master forced Scorpius to step forward, until he saw the ring laying in the dukessa's outstretched palm.

66

He couldn't stop himself from looking into the dukessa's eyes. His young master's mother returned his gaze, eyes shining with emotion. Scorpius knelt before her once more, extending his hand so she could place the ring upon his middle finger.

The rectangular black onyx, in a silver setting resembling plumes of wind or smoke, lay along the base of his finger to the knuckle. A strange sense of well-being came over him, as though his hand had always longed for the weight of this stone upon it.

As he turned his hand slightly, the carving within the onyx revealed itself — a dragon in flight. The sound of the dragon's wings filled his mind, raising the hair along the back of his neck. At just that moment, the dukessa wrapped her fingers around his jeweled hand and calmed him.

Scorpius bowed his head. "Your Grace."

"You have returned my son to me. The joy you bring cannot be truly expressed. Not really."

Another subtle nudge from Lord Thibault helped Scorpius rise to his feet. The girls surged forward to take up his hand and admire the ring.

"Have you showed Scorpius his new home?"

"We went to my father straight away, and then to you," Lord Thibault said.

"You must show him the estate and grounds, then, but take a guard with you."

"Yes, Mother," his master said, leaning close to kiss the dukessa warmly upon the cheek.

"May I come, too?" the boy said, suddenly forlorn.

"Hurry, then," Lord Thibault said, already striding from the room. Scorpius bowed deeply and backed away as the boy dashed past him.

Catching up to his master easily, Scorpius fought the urge to gaze at the hand that now wore a ring such as he'd never imagined. It turned his falconer's clothing into shabby rags, but no doubt that would be remedied before he turned in for the night.

As he hung back from the sight of the two brothers delighting in one another's company, the younger one skipping along and dragging on Lord Thibault's hand, Scorpius felt the keen loss of Richolf.

A part of him didn't want to think of his former master ever again. Yet that would be an insult too horrible to contemplate.

He would just have to learn to live with the stabbing ache that erupted inside of him from time to time, wouldn't he? He had done so as a boy, even younger than his master's brother. He'd learned to live with the loss of the parents who'd never come for him, as the duke and dukessa had come for Lord Thibault when it was time for him to leave the nursery.

They passed through gleaming corridors, polished and smooth enough to slide upon, which the boy did with practiced ease. They rounded corners and skipped down staircases, made their way through galleries and ducked through servants' entries. Staff stepped artfully out of the way as the brothers raced for the door to the grounds.

Scorpius trotted to keep up, crossing the threshold into the sunny afternoon. He paused to take in the small village of outbuildings and servants behind the estate, which was impressive enough. As he jogged ahead to rejoin his master and his master's brother, he saw they crested a small slope that opened onto an ornate garden and revealed rolling parkland beyond.

Lord Thibault turned to smile at him. Scorpius fought the sense of betrayal towards his former master, the falconer, for his heart soared with the sense that he had finally come home.

67

Scorpius' sharp cry ricocheted through the stone gallery, his hand pinned by the sword master's boot, the pommel grinding into his hand.

A kick to his leg knocked his feet from under him. Slamming to the ground, he lost his numb grip upon the sword. An iron grip encircled his throat, choking him, just as the merciless tip of a blade hovered over his eye.

All he could do was stare down the length of steel into the swordmaster's cool gaze.

With a grunt, the older man thrust Scorpius from him and stalked away. Pressing hard against the wall for support, Scorpius bent, coughing. Sweat rolled into his eyes.

"Again."

With barely enough time to lift his head, Scorpius saw the swordmaster bearing down on him, weapon raised over his head. A chill gripped Scorpius' limbs. In two strides the man was upon him. All he could do was roll and scramble to his feet, his sword lying too far away.

The other man whirled to keep Scorpius in his sights, already lunging forward, the sword blocking his escape route. So he dove under it, sliding along the smooth floor, rolling once more towards his blade.

Scorpius was sure he heard a curse as he scooped up the pommel and regained his feet. A surge of purpose burst up through his chest, clearing his head so that he had the chance to think, though his body moved with all the speed he could muster.

Just in time, Scorpius braced himself with both hands on the pommel. The swordmaster brought his blade down in a bone-jarring arc, the steel ringing in the gallery. Laboring hard to meet the man's powerful blows, Scorpius gave ground, stepping carefully backward, trying to stay free of the wall.

Panting hard, Scorpius blinked against the sweat but dared not let go of the pommel. The swordmaster suddenly charged forward, pulling back when Scorpius moved to parry. With a lunge and a twist, the older man threw Scorpius down at his feet, knocking the wind from his chest.

Gasping at the painful pressure in his lungs, Scorpius watched the swordmaster kick his sword away for a second time. Once again he lay pinned beneath the older man's boot until the breath burned back into him.

Once again, the only thing he could do was return the swordmaster's gaze. This time, the cool stare warmed into a spark of respect.

The older man dipped his head in a salute, lifting his foot from Scorpius' chest, bending to offer a hand of assistance.

Scorpius rose just as his master, Lord Thibault crossed the gallery to join them.

"A falconer's boy, you say?" the swordmaster said.

"Yes, sir." Scorpius still gripped his weapon as though the other man might press on with more training. His master arrived instead, to give him a hearty swat on the back.

"I told you he'd be worth the trouble," Lord Thibault said, his smile wide.

"He's got size, and he's got speed. Often there is one but not the other." The swordmaster looked Scorpius up and down. He drew up as tall as he could.

"If he is to serve me, he must protect me," his master said, addressing the older man but looking at Scorpius.

"He is accustomed to serving birds of prey, my lord. They have taught him to read the lay of the land, to move with assurance, to be ready."

The swordmaster closed the distance between himself and Scorpius, coming nose to nose, which forced him to look up slightly. He remained just as intimidating. "You are used to letting the birds do the killing. Do you have what it takes?"

Scorpius glanced over at his master, who watched with a slight air of uncertainty. Though the swordmaster's rank was a servant of this noble house, in the matter of whether he would agree to train Scorpius, it appeared Lord Thibault was prepared to defer to the man who ruled in this domain.

Scorpius didn't know how the idea came to him, but when it struck, he knew he must carry it through.

Without warning, Scorpius thrust the pommel of his sword up and out, clipping the swordmaster on the chin, putting the older man off-balance. Scorpius charged forward, using his superior weight to pin the man to the floor.

He was just maneuvering his blade to hold it across the swordmaster's throat, when the older man grabbed Scorpius' arm, thrust hard to the side and rolled them both over. The swordmaster was like a snake, wrapped tightly around Scorpius' arms and legs.

A sharp blow to his arm forced his numbed hand to drop the blade. A knee to his gut forced a cry from him.

For a brief instant, Scorpius saw the fierce glow of the kill flash through the swordmaster's eyes. It passed just as quickly.

The intense pressure eased off, and the older man released him, gazing down with the slightest suggestion of admiration. "That's a start," he said.

68

"My father has asked for you," Lord Thibault said in an offhanded way, dismounting from his horse.

A groom moved forward, taking hold of the reins as Scorpius slid smoothly out of the saddle. He dropped to his feet, trying to catch his master's eye.

"Yes, my lord," he said, following behind, dread rolling heavily through his guts. They left the sunshine and the carefree afternoon behind, heading into the cool stone passageway at a brisk pace.

His master led Scorpius to his own room, where a new set of clothes had been laid out on his bed and a basin of fresh water awaited. Lord Thibault supervised every aspect of Scorpius' preparations, fussing over him like a valet over a bridegroom.

"You mustn't worry," Lord Thibault said, tying his sleeves into place with care.

"I won't, my lord."

"I have already informed my father that you will serve as my man." He grabbed Scorpius by the shoulders and turned him toward the door. "The duke must accept you as my acquisition."

Scorpius nodded, heart leaping as his master nudged him forward. Only when they were both out in the corridor did Lord Thibault take his habitual lead.

"My brother, the markiisi chose his own man, and I am now of an age to do the same."

"He will not be pleased, I take it, my lord." Scorpius recalled the dark chuckles of his master's uncle and the guard captain at mention of the duke. As they rounded a corner and the gallery widened to a polished grandeur, Scorpius fought to still his fear.

"He means to assess the damage, so to speak. See what faith he has in me."

Scorpius recognized the double doors from their first meeting with the duke. Servants pulled with practiced ease at the golden handles, stepping back as the doors swung open. It was all happening too fast. Scorpius and his master stood before the duke and there was nothing for it but to bow deeply and sweep his arm to his chest.

He straightened only to catch a glimpse of Lord Thibault backing away and striding back through the doors, which closed with a smart click behind him. A flash freeze seemed to stop Scorpius' blood in its tracks.

"Step forward."

Scorpius forced himself to move, crossing the carpet which was soft as flower petals. He got as near to the duke as he dared, his gaze solidly averted.

"Where did he find you?"

"Your son arrived at my master's — my former master's — cottage for a hunt. I served a falconer, Your Grace."

From the corner of his eye, he saw the chancellor standing once again at a respectful distance.

"So there are none to recommend you." The satisfaction at this glaring lack made Scorpius shrivel inside.

"Could we not pay this falconer a visit, Your Grace?" the chancellor said.

Was Scorpius prohibited from speaking without first having been spoken to? Why didn't Lord Thibault take as great care with these few simple rules as he'd done with this jerkin?

"To which estate were you attached?" the duke asked.

"To the House of Razlava, Your Grace. You will not find my master — you will not find the falconer there. Lord Thibault sent him away."

"Did he?" The duke strode forward. Scorpius had grown accustomed to being the tallest person in any room, but Lord Thibault's father matched him and more. Everything inside Scorpius cried out to back away, but he recalled his master's words: *The duke must accept you as my acquisition.*

He remembered the shrieks of that poor young guard, flogged by Lord Dirske during the Nightmare Hunt. Was this duke prone to similar outbursts? Why else would his master's uncle and the guard captain have laughed so?

Then he remembered how the guard captain had expected

to find the scars of similar floggings across Scorpius' back. Forcing himself to hold his ground as the duke looked him over, Scorpius bit back the words that wanted to tumble in explanation from his lips.

"You saved his life," said Lord Thibault's father. "Yet who put him in jeopardy? No one to speak for you. No one but the grateful lord you now serve."

No one but Ingerith, his former master's lover, whose identity must remain secret.

Scorpius swallowed hard, glancing up to see the chancellor staring intently at him. "Your son showed great mercy to my master, Your Grace," Scorpius said, his mouth dry with fear. "As my master showed always to me."

"Thank the gods that Thibault is only a second son." The duke turned away, heading for the doors. Scorpius' face flushed hot on behalf of his new master.

"I shall leave you to it," the duke said, striding out into the gallery.

Scorpius straightened from his bow to meet the appraising glance of the chancellor, whose gaze took in everything, whose expression gave away nothing.

69

"Do you dance?"

"No..." Scorpius stumbled over what to call the chancellor. Why, oh why did Lord Thibault neglect to mention these little details before abandoning him here in the duke's drawing room? "No, sir," he said, certain that wasn't right.

A fleeting smile grazed the chancellor's lips. "'No, my lord.'"

Scorpius bowed slightly, face flushing hot. "No, my lord."

The chancellor moved closer, so discreetly that Scorpius started. "Your former master, the falconer, never took you to a fête?"

"Ah..."

The chancellor folded his arms across his chest. "How many dinner guests would you suppose attended your largest dinner party?"

Scorpius thought back to the outdoor lunch they'd enjoyed in the forest — Richolf, Ingerith, Alegreza and himself. Where were they, now? "Just three, my lord."

"Three, including yourself?"

"Four, my lord." Scorpius shifted his body slightly to keep this man in his sights. He felt like he was circling the swordmaster.

"Do you ride?"

There was no point in puffing himself up. This chancellor would see through that in a blink. "Not well. Just enough to keep from falling off, really, my lord."

Again, the barest of smiles. "What did Lord Thibault tell you when he brought you here?"

"That I would be his man, my lord." Scorpius drew himself up, daring to look into the chancellor's eyes. He hadn't the slightest idea if it was forbidden. However, a lord's man must be bold.

"Do you even have a suspicion as to what that entails?" The chancellor gazed at him with a strange mixture of hope and distain.

A jumble of memories crowded Scorpius' mind. The nobles who'd come to the falconer's cottage for the hunt, some with a retinue of courtiers, some with harsh words and blows, some with laughter and wineskins. The depravity of the Nightmare Hunt chilled him now, recalling how they'd all served Lord Dirske, no matter how wretched it had felt to do so.

"I do, my lord."

The chancellor turned and walked towards the ornate desk. "The duke has doubts that you are up to the task." He turned and regarded Scorpius, the hint of kindness in his eyes giving Scorpius the heart to press on.

"The falconer fetched me from the nursery, my lord."

Eyebrows raising only slightly, the chancellor said, "Did he?"

"While I was a small boy, I was treated as a noble. After that, I was trained to serve them." He shrugged at the oddity of his own life.

"As Lord Thibault's man, you will need to ride," the chancellor said. "You will need to wield a blade. You will need to do both things better than he does. You must protect him at every hour of the day. You cannot leave his side for long. You must attend the same dinners, cut figures at the same dances."

Closing the distance between them, the chancellor looked deeply for something as he gazed for several moments upon Scorpius. "The duke has doubts about you," he repeated.

Scorpius bristled inside. The duke had barely glanced at him. Richolf had trusted him. Richolf had saved him from turning into... only the gods knew.

He felt the outrage flowing through him. The chancellor nodded, as if engaged in an internal conversation.

"I do not," he said. "You will be trained, and Lord Thibault will have his man." Turning away, the chancellor slipped into the shadows of the vast drawing room, just as Scorpius noticed the double doors swinging open behind him, as if by some silent command.

Though apparently gone, Scorpius felt he had to acknowledge the man whose opinion had been the deciding factor. "My lord," he said, bowing smartly to thin air. Then he turned and left the drawing room behind, nearly failing to nod at the servants standing at each side of the doorway.

70

The falcon stared at him from the gloom of the mews, its thin body painful to look at. As Scorpius hurried past the red-tail, the gray and the king hawk, the expected tiny lilting of bells attached to their jesses never came. Instead, the birds stood unmoving upon their perches, following his passage with their burning golden eyes.

Scorpius called for the dog, listening hard for that telltale loping *swoosh* through the grass. Rounding the corner of the cottage, he broke into a run, needing to see Richolf. Hurling himself at the door, he yanked and rattled the door latch but it wouldn't open.

"Master!" he called.

Something grabbed his attention over the pounding of his heart — it was the dog, whining and crying from around the side of the cottage. "I'm coming!" he called, shoving past brush and tearing his fine new clothes.

He'd been certain the dog was just around the corner, but there was only the boarded-up window where Ingerith had once stolen into the cottage in order to save Lord Thibault's life. Scorpius used his newly-honed strength gained from the sword training, but nothing would free the boards keeping him out of the cottage where he'd grown to young manhood.

The dog's cries led him all around the cottage, where he tried every window with no success. His new doublet now in shreds, Scorpius winced as a thorny branch sliced through to the skin.

Stepping away from the stone wall, squeezing through more brush, he hissed in pain as his trouser leg ripped. His hand pressed on the tear, slick with blood, while an irritating *snap*, *snap*, *snap* filled the air as he cleared the tangle of branches at last.

Scorpius turned to look for the dog. Instead, he found the red-tail, the gray and the king hawk strewn along the path he'd just taken. Their crushed bodies were smeared with blood.

Recoiling, Scorpius found every falcon dead, covering the

clearing in front of the cottage.

"Master!" he screamed. "Master!"

Two hands gripped his arms. He tried to sit up, but twisted blankets held him fast.

"Scorpius!" Lord Thibault said. "I'm here. Hush, now — you'll have the other servants running down here in a minute."

"We have to get them out. They're dying!"

"Who are?"

"The hawks," Scorpius said, his mouth so dry he could barely speak.

"The hawks," his master repeated, slowly releasing him.

Scorpius peeled the blankets away, sitting up to run trembling hands through his hair. "They're still tied to their perches, inside the mews. They can't get out on their own. They're starving. Why should they die because I'm here with you?"

The words were out of his mouth before he realized the tone he'd taken with his master. He scrambled to his knees in the bed among the strewn bedding, bowing his head low.

Lord Thibault placed a steadying hand on Scorpius' arm.

"Forgive me, lord."

"It's forgotten." He stood, heading for the door that separated their chambers. "Most of it, anyway."

71

Scorpius strode briskly through the servants' entrance and into the warm afternoon. He'd been summoned to meet Lord Thibault at the stables, which likely meant a wild ride before dinner.

Still barely more than a novice when it came to riding, Scorpius deeply wished he'd somehow found the time to go out on his own before being called to accompany his skilled master. With all of the weapons training, learning his way around the vast estate, meeting all of the family members, staff and servants, Scorpius had barely time to blink. He'd never found that elusive moment, never placed his boot in the stirrup, because truth be known, he wished he never had to mount another horse.

A boyhood spent among the hawks and hunting dogs had given him a strong rapport with animals. He could read the behavior of the powerful stallions his master favored.

They sensed his unease around them, and since no horse respected a timid rider, every mount he'd been given fought his commands that weren't commands at all. As Scorpius neared the stables, his stomach knotted up inside.

Couldn't today have been dancing day? He was a quick study in the music room, much to Lord Thibault's teasing delight.

The smells of the stables assaulted his nostrils as he entered through the wide doorway. At the far end, leaning against a post, his master gazed affectionately down at something squirming in the hay, just beyond the stall divider.

Forcing himself to join his master, taking care not to allow his distaste for riding show on his face or in his demeanor, Scorpius rounded the post and nodded at Lord Thibault, glancing over at the straw and at what lay upon it.

For a moment, he didn't understand the sharp, piercing joy flooding his chest. A moment later, Scorpius lay flattened by the weight of Richolf's hunting dog. Wriggling in greeting, tongue licking every speck of exposed skin, the dog cried its happiness.

When he could wrestle his face clear of the dog, he gazed at his master in wonder.

Lord Thibault laughed. "I sent someone out to check on the place. Apparently there's a new falconer in residence. No need to worry over the birds. They're being well taken care of."

Scorpius wrapped his arms around the dog and squeezed. He couldn't contain the excited animal, which set to work licking his face and ear with renewed vigor. "How did you...?"

"I simply sent a reminder that the dog belonged not to the cottage, but to the man who previously held the position there," Lord Thibault said.

"Is that true?" Scorpius asked, leaning his face into the familiar softness of the dog's fur.

"I haven't the slightest idea, but that's what the servant told him."

Scorpius laughed, falling backwards into the hay under the onslaught of the dog's attentions.

A bed was made for the dog. Some food was found. Scorpius tore himself away to accompany his master to dinner in the great hall.

Late in the night, when he tossed and turned upon the smooth sheets, Scorpius made up his mind to rejoin his beloved companion even if he was forbidden entry to the manor house. He crept past Lord Thibault's rhythmic breathing, navigated the polished floors in stocking feet and hurried out of the entry way as though duty compelled him.

Curling up in the hay beside his dog, Scorpius fell into the deepest sleep he could remember in years.

72

Pulling free of the girl's sleepy grip, Scorpius slid from under the covers, rummaging for his trousers.

His master lay sprawled in the arms of last night's amusement, who now snored with indelicate persistence. The gray shadows warned of dawn. Time to be off.

Slipping outside to be sure the horses were saddled and ready, Scorpius returned to the slaves' hut, ignoring the gaze of the older woman, now roused from her mat on the floor. She sat and watched him as he tapped Lord Thibault on the temple.

He hadn't been able to make out whether she was the girls' mother, or just someone who lived here with them. She said nothing as his master groaned loudly and stretched.

Neither girl awoke as Lord Thibault stumbled into his clothes, but the older woman's gaze followed Scorpius as he prodded and cajoled his master to the door. As Lord Thibault shook the night off and placed his foot in the stirrup, Scorpius crept back to the woman's side and knelt beside her.

"For your hospitality," he said, placing a kerchief bundle in her hand. The aroma of spiced cakes filled the small space, bringing a surprised smile to the woman's lips. Ducking out into the dew-heavy morning, Scorpius swung up into the saddle and nudged his horse forward with the heels of his boots.

Catching up with his master, Scorpius waited for the grin he knew Lord Thibault would flash at him.

"Determined to keep me on schedule," his master said.

"If I do not, I shall catch it from the chancellor."

"Remind me to somehow lace your drink with a sleeping draught next time, would you?"

"I shall do my best, my lord."

"You shall do your best for the chancellor and not for your master," Lord Thibault said, turning back to look at the slave hut with longing.

"He serves your house, as do I, my lord." Scorpius had already pushed the slave girl from his mind. Her kisses and caresses had been ordered, making him long for their own rooms and a hot bath.

"Can we refrain from mentioning my illustrious house, just at present?" Lord Thibault twisted back to gaze at the road that would take them home. "I shall be back in its clutches soon enough."

They rode for a time in silence, the swaying gaits of their mounts the only thing to break the stillness of the morning.

"Do you know, when I first met you at the falconer's, you gave no indication whatsoever that you would ruin lovely mornings like this one," his master said.

Scorpius snorted derisively.

"And I went out of my way to find a sweet little thing for you to enjoy."

"Your generosity is never in question, my lord. Merely your punctuality."

"Who is asking for me at this time of day?" Lord Thibault said, sober realization dawning in his face.

"What do you take me for?" Scorpius said. "You shall find out only after I have you bathed and dressed."

"Why did you let me drink so much? I feel like death."

"One might imagine you'd tire of it, in time," Scorpius said.

"Weren't you drinking?" his master said. "Why do you look so presentable?"

"One of us has to keep his head." His horse wanted to challenge his master's, but that would not be tolerated as they neared the estate. He held his mount back to follow Lord Thibault's horse just slightly.

"By the gods," his master chuckled. "I'm a slave to my man."

"You merely serve your house, my lord," Scorpius said. "As do I."

73

Scorpius readied himself to follow Lord Thibault to an audience before the dukessa as two slaves drew open the ornate doors. The slightest of movements caught his eye, and he halted, grip ready upon his sword.

In place of a rival to strike down his master on his mother's doorstep, the duke's chancellor nodded quietly from the shadows, summoning Scorpius with the merest flick of his head.

Meeting Lord Thibault's questioning gaze, Scorpius took a step back and bowed his apologies as his master was swept forward into his mother's drawing room, doors closing behind him.

Striding across the corridor, Scorpius joined the chancellor who ducked into a hidden doorway. Keeping pace with the duke's advisor, Scorpius moved along the dim servants' passageway, dodging staff going swiftly about their business.

They did not speak until they entered the chancellor's private offices. No slaves here to open doors, so once the older man made his way to the desk, Scorpius turned and shut the doors behind him.

"Please sit down," the chancellor said.

The tiniest seed of alarm settled inside Scorpius' gut. Still, he made his way to the chair across from the desk and sat as if he had nothing to worry about.

"The dukessa is delivering news your master will not welcome, I'm afraid," the chancellor said.

The older man fought a smile, which calmed the swirling in Scorpius' chest. Forcing his limbs to affect an ease he did not feel, Scorpius said, "He can withstand it, I am sure, my Lord Chancellor."

"The dukessa will inform him that she has a stable of beauties handpicked for Lord Thibault's perusal, beginning with this coming season," the chancellor said.

Scorpius thought of his master, how he'd left the latest girl's arms only hours before. "My master won't take such an order very gracefully, I'm afraid."

"No. Of course, there *is* something that will soften the blow for my young lord. Do see that he gets this." The chancellor leaned forward and passed a small folded note into Scorpius' hand.

"Do I need to know what this is?" Scorpius asked.

"It's a list of courtesans."

Scorpius' skin prickled with warning. "Courtesans."

"The very best." The chancellor smiled a generous smile, as though he could speak from experience.

Tucking the note into his jerkin, Scorpius smiled back. "I'll see that he gets it."

"If we let the dukessa match-make as she pleases, she'll be content for a time, and Lord Thibault can find his own love match from among my contacts."

"Can he not search for someone whose name makes neither list, my Lord Chancellor?"

Again, a broad smile. "I know he's often done so. I've gathered the information I needed in order to match his preferences to my list."

Scorpius thought of the slaves they'd bedded last night. Did they report to the chancellor? Perhaps the older woman who'd stayed on her mat?

"Nothing escapes your notice, does it, my Lord Chancellor?"

The older man's smile dimmed, but in a thoughtful manner, sizing up Scorpius as if in a new light. "It is my life's work to take note of most everything," he said.

74

Already bathed and attired in his most tasteful doublet, Scorpius threw his master a linen to dry himself as Lord Thibault rose dripping from the water.

"I don't know why she's in such a scorching hurry." His master scrubbed his hair back and forth until it stood on end. Stepping onto the soft mat beside his carefully arranged garments, Lord Thibault held his arms out so the slave could dry him off.

"Apparently, that is the way of mothers, my lord," Scorpius said, leaning against his master's bedposts, arms crossed before him. "Even the mothers of villagers and what-have-you."

The slave drew a comb through the master's hair. "And just what was so crucial at that precise moment that you left me to my mother's scheming, utterly unprotected?" Lord Thibault asked.

"Do I not serve the chancellor before I serve my lord?" Scorpius watched as the slave deftly clothed their master in fine hose, hand-worked linen and breeches cut to display Lord Thibault's form as future sire of noble lineage.

Sulking darkly, Lord Thibault shrugged into a velvet doublet sparkling with silver stitching and gem stones.

"Permission to speak freely?" Scorpius asked.

"No," Lord Thibault said, walking to the bench where he sat to be fitted with elaborate shoes. "You do not have my permission to speak freely, because I know what you're going to say."

Unfolding his arms to stand respectfully, Scorpius inclined his head slightly. "My lord."

The slave pushed gingerly to slip the shoe on their master's foot, taking care not to press too hard on the encrusted gem work.

"You're going to tell me to stop being such a simpleton and at least have a look at these noble ladies before I reject them, simply because my mother has made a list of them. I still have a choice in all of this, do I not?"

"As far as I understand it, my lord."

His master rose, shaking his head. "It's my choice until my father informs me which one of them will be my mate." Again spreading his arms wide, Lord Thibault stood as the slave buckled a ceremonial sword around his hips, draping a sash across one shoulder and fixing it with a jeweled clasp.

"You say the village mothers do this same thing to their progeny?"

"As far as I can work it out, my lord, they may chose whomsoever they wish, as long as the bride is one which the mother approves."

"I suppose it's entirely possible that there are ladies on the dukessa's list who are convinced I am not a suitable choice for them." Lord Thibault adjusted his sash and sword belt to suit his own taste, now that the slave had stepped aside.

"Without permission to speak freely, my lord, I would have to say that is highly unlikely."

His master took a deep breath before leading the way into the corridor. "I don't know why you should be so unkind to me today. Really, Scorpius, I could use cheering up."

Keeping pace with his master, their footsteps striking the polished floor in unison, Scorpius dipped a hand into the fold of his doublet. He pulled the chancellor's note free and offered it to Lord Thibault.

His gaze searching Scorpius for clues, Lord Thibault checked his pace only slightly as he opened the note and glanced at its contents. Then he stopped walking and faced Scorpius head on.

"Another list?" his master said, grinning.

"The dukessa knows none of these, I think."

"The chancellor's list."

"His indeed, my lord."

Lord Thibault tucked the note away, deep in the recesses of his velvet doublet. Continuing along the corridor, his master's step grew lighter. "Look at us, Scorpius. We're ridiculous."

"Just for a few hours, my lord. Then we can shed all of this, and perhaps gentle hands will aid us in that endeavor."

75

Scorpius and his master waded into the sea of expectant faces, all craning to have a good look at the noble with his head on the marriage block.

The dukessa's reception was so well attended, it was now something of a crush. His heart rate accelerating, Scorpius kept one hand on the pommel of his sword. He'd never faced such a potential mob as Lord Thibault's man. Anyone could lurk in this press of silk and velvet.

There was no way to stick close enough to his master in order to protect him while maintaining a respectful distance. As the other young nobles swarmed ahead to greet the guest of honor, Scorpius was forced to stand shoulder to shoulder with his master, something that would not have been tolerated at any other time.

Thanking the gods for his extra height in these circumstances, Scorpius kept his gaze roaming the crowd for anything out of the ordinary. Of course, the duke had dispatched the household guard, who were liberally sprinkled amongst the servants and slaves. Their assured presence felt like a calm hand upon his shoulder.

As young ladies exhibiting their finer charms made their way forward, Scorpius forced himself to stop sharing sideways glances with his master as they made silent comment on the various matrimonial candidates. Instead, he made eye contact from guard to guard, nodding as they indicated all was well.

It was a relief when Lord Thibault finally sat down to eat. Standing behind his master's chair, Scorpius had a far better vantage point from which to scan the hall. From here he could see which heads tilted together for private conversation, which ladies eyed his master with undisguised hunger and which drew back in disinterest.

It became clear, as they waited for the meal-tasting slaves to finish their portions, that a particular young lady was holding gazes for a considerable time with Lord Thibault. Both the chancellor and the dukessa had noted the exchanges from their perch in the gallery overlooking the hall, if their whispered consultations meant what Scorpius thought they meant.

From the expression Lord Thibault's mother displayed, Scorpius knew the lovely lady in question met with official approval. As for the chancellor, he was much too far away for Scorpius to read the subtleties.

Besides, something else had begun to pull his attention to the far corner of the hall.

Several of the guard had posted themselves near a small group of nobles who managed to stand out from the rest, even in this finely turned-out company. Three males and one female, as richly attired as anyone else, yet something about their demeanor felt at odds. Scorpius' senses sharpened to a knife edge.

The nearest door was a dozen strides away.

His best choice was to push Lord Thibault beneath the solid banquet table and cover him with his body while the guard took action, as he knew they would. Now that he'd worked out a plan, he fanned his fingers over his sword pommel and stood poised to spring.

Still, the eating and conversation continued, laughter pealing up over the coiffures as though nothing simmered in the afternoon air.

Somehow the young woman from the little knot of suspicious nobles had caught his master's eye. This time, it was impossible not to notice Lord Thibault's interest in the exotic lady, even when he could not see his master's face.

Wasn't she a beauty? Her skin was a shade darker than most other ladies', her eyes alight with tracery that brought out an irresistible wildness. Her hair was well-concealed beneath a scarf and hat arrangement that only served to make Scorpius long to tug at them both, to see her locks tumble free.

The more eligible young lady continued to engage his master with glances and conversation. The dukessa continued to smile discreetly upon her son from the gallery. However, the chancellor followed Scorpius' focus upon the unknown nobles and the interest shown them by the guard.

Scorpius tried to read the chancellor's signals, but the older man was too schooled in deception to give anything away. All he could do was be ready to draw his sword if it came to that. Even if that meant striking down the most beautiful woman he'd ever seen.

76

It was a blessing that Scorpius had taken to dancing so readily. Keeping one eye trained to the next figure in the promenade, while the other eye scanned the room — in particular the other dancers — was no small task.

No less distracting was the exotic beauty who'd obviously captured Lord Thibault's notice. To his master's credit, Lord Thibault spread his charmed responses equally among the assembled young ladies. Not even the fair-haired favorite of the dukessa and the chancellor could suspect what Scorpius knew with certainty.

By the time the night gave way to dawn and the guests made their yawning reverences to Lord Thibault and the dukessa, Scorpius bristled with the need for sleep. Yet there would be none, as Lord Thibault brushed past him briefly to conceal a murmured request.

Scorpius fought to conceal his expression, unable to prevent himself glancing through the crowd toward her.

The mysterious one's retinue didn't miss Scorpius' interest. He saw how they reached subtly for their sword hilts.

Lord Thibault strode forward to take his delighted mother's hands in his, bending his head to kiss her cheek and leaving Scorpius to devise a means of stopping the unknown beauty from departing. How was he to arrange a decidedly unofficial meeting with her when her kinsmen never left her side?

Scorpius forced himself to walk toward them, still unsure of how he would phrase his master's request. He saw the men fan out slightly around their prize, standing as tall as they could, broadening their stances. He judged from their reaction to his approach that it was he who held the upper hand, and slowed his pace accordingly.

Once he stood before the mysterious one, Scorpius felt the pull of her allure like a lethal undertow. He quickly dropped his gaze, unwilling to look into those violet eyes. Taking her hand in his, he bowed and kissed her knuckles.

"My Lord Thibault requests that you stroll with me into the garden," Scorpius said. "He regrets that the evening sped by so quickly that he was unable to get to know you... better."

The young lady curtsied to him with an aggressive movement unlike any other lady present. Her guard also bowed quickly to him. Imagine it. As easy as that.

Striding toward a far doorway, leaving his master to chuckle and quip with the last of the departing guests, Scorpius led the exotic beauty and her kinsmen into the dew-chilled air. The sky lightened in gray warning.

Their steps echoed on the empty flagstones, their path twisting farther into the recesses of the garden. Scorpius ignored the tightness in his gut as he wiped the stone bench dry. The mysterious one settled herself to wait. It didn't take long.

When Lord Thibault arrived, Scorpius and the lady's retinue stepped into the shadows with one accord. Glancing back at his master, Scorpius' breath caught in his chest as he saw Lord Thibault's hands slip the young lady's headpiece and scarf aside.

Tumbling free, the mysterious one's hair wasn't simply dark, or fiery, or fair as Scorpius had longed to discover. No, her locks fell in black and white stripes such as he had never seen before.

Turning to the men surrounding him, he saw now that each one also hid his hair beneath a scarf and cap. In their gazes Scorpius saw ferocious pride in the secret he now held about them.

The young lady returned Lord Thibault's kisses and embraces with matching ardor. Scorpius hoped his master knew what he was doing. Wordlessly, Scorpius raised one finger to his eye and then swept his hand toward the estate grounds.

The men turned and kept watch while Scorpius kept his eye on Lord Thibault and his lady. It would be hours yet before Scorpius saw his bed, and even then, how would he rest when this was where his master determined to lead them?

77

Scorpius sank down upon the hay, arms gathering up his dog as he closed his eyes against the graying sky. He hadn't realized he'd slept until two booted feet stopped in the hay beside his head.

Instantly awake, he grabbed for his knife but only managed to cut his hand along the edge of the sword that had anticipated his move. When he heard the dog growl, Scorpius barked the command to stay, sick at the knowledge that he might have delivered the animal's death sentence.

A chuckle soon dispelled that fear — only to replace it with the hair-prickling realization that these were the chancellor's boots and sword.

"You only come out here when you're troubled," the chancellor said.

"My Lord Chancellor," Scorpius said, pulling himself to his knees.

"Bring the dog." The older man turned and strode from stables, barely rustling the straw. Scorpius gazed over at his former master's hunting dog, crouching at the ready but awaiting his signal. No wonder he ran to him when he needed solace. They understood each other.

Trotting to catch up, Scorpius pressed a kerchief to his hand to stop the bleeding.

"You have reason to be troubled," the chancellor said when they were out of range of eyes or ears from the stables and storage huts. The only sound was their footsteps over the forested path as they made their way into the trees left unshaped by the gardeners.

Scorpius tried to form a way of saying why he'd done nothing but lay there all night staring into the gloom while his master slept soundly. There was no way of doing so without betraying Lord Thibault's trust.

Finally they came to a sheltered grove with an overturned tree that the chancellor sat upon. Scorpius stood before him with the dog at heel. A sense of dread warred with the curiosity inside him.

"Your master has made no advances toward the young lady who showed interest at the ball."

"He knows she meets with the dukessa's approval, my Lord Chancellor. And yours."

"Then why does he meet with the Sibian?"

Scorpius' heart seemed to stop beating. Yet he took in a steadying breath. He must not falter before the chancellor. "Why do you think, my lord?"

The chancellor blinked and looked away. "This is most unexpected."

The memory of the young lady's edge of ferocity when compared to the other prospective brides brought a wry smile to Scorpius' face. "It isn't really, my lord."

Training his gaze upon Scorpius, the chancellor's own worry lined his face in a way Scorpius had never witnessed before. It flooded Scorpius with a desire to reassure the older man, though speaking for his master was folly.

"You have been very discreet," the chancellor said. "I have merely been doing this longer than you have."

Scorpius bowed in acknowledgment.

"You must tell me if you think your master intends to ask for her hand."

"What would happen if he did?"

"Our dominion and Sibiu have been at odds for fifteen generations," the chancellor said. "I don't know why her name was approved for the guest list."

"Who else could have approved it except you, my lord?"

Scorpius watched in fascination as the older man paled and looked away.

78

Reaching up, the chancellor pulled his hat free from his head, revealing stubbly growth instead of full locks of hair. Scorpius' pulse quickened in alarm that the duke's advisor should perform such a deferential gesture before him. Turning swiftly to be certain there was no one approaching, Scorpius rounded on the chancellor, whose head bowed as he stared at the ground between them.

In the growing light, the striped pattern emerged to spill its secrets, even in the closely cropped stubble.

It was all Scorpius could do to stifle the gasp that choked him. "You, my lord?" he said.

The chancellor's gaze lifted to bore into Scorpius' own.

"You approved her name on the guest list," Scorpius said.

"It's time to take chances," the chancellor said as if begging forgiveness.

Scorpius turned and covered his mouth with his hand, as if the tumult of questions inside him threatened to spill out like a bout of sickness. He felt the chancellor close the gap between them. Scorpius' skin prickled at keeping his back turned to such a noble, but turning now would force him to graze the chancellor's body. He straightened instead.

The years since he was a small boy, newly arrived at the falconer's as his apprentice, fell away as Scorpius recalled what had happened to his former master. Richolf had been witness to secrets over which the nobles were only too willing to kill one another. Possessing those secrets had led to screams, nightmares and wounds that never healed.

Now Scorpius knew that the chancellor belonged to the Sibiu people. His body trembled as he stood with the noble a hair's breadth behind him. His hand still stung from the cut the chancellor had given him upon awakening.

"It's only fair that you should know something about me," the noble said. "For I know something about you. Something that could change your life in ways you once only dreamed of."

Scorpius' heart beat so fast he felt unsteady. "My lord," he whispered.

"The young lady whose approval has been given by the dukessa and myself is from a well-placed family to the north, whose grandsire will be arriving after the next moon to collect her. And to make arrangements if the duke so desires to make an alliance between their houses."

It was hard for Scorpius to concentrate on the chancellor's words, his pulse surged so loudly in his ears.

"I will arrange for you to attend me when the duke calls an audience with her grandsire," said the chancellor. "Then you may see for yourself what sort of family this man represents."

Did he mean for Scorpius to scout the terrain between the noble houses on behalf of his master Lord Thibault? Or did he mean what Scorpius' pounding heartbeat suggested?

"All families have faces they show to the world, and faces they protect. Injured sides, shameful sides, monstrous sides. Some families have mysteries, never solved. Until someone uncovers just the right shape to solve the puzzle."

The chancellor stepped around Scorpius to stand before him. "You will report to me regarding your master's involvement with the Sibiu, and in return, I will ensure you're in the drawing room when the lady's grandsire arrives. Agreed?"

Bowing and sweeping a hand toward his heart in reverence, Scorpius said, "Agreed, my lord." He remained bowed until the chancellor placed his hat once more upon his head, turned and strode back towards the gardens.

79

"Whatever is the matter with you, Scorpius?" said Lord Thibault.

They strode down the long gallery, handing off their practise blades to a servant. Both of them were in need of fresh clothes and a bath, and struck off for their rooms.

Only their footsteps answered his master's question as Scorpius rummaged through his customary excuses. Today, however, they slipped stubbornly from his grasp.

"Perhaps you'd like to take a few hours for yourself this afternoon," the young noble said.

"With no one to guard you?" Scorpius gave a derisive laugh. "Then who should guard me from your father's displeasure?" They rounded the corner and jogged up the stairs.

"I knew there was something odd about you today," Lord Thibault said. "You know my father doesn't give the hind end of a pack horse for my amusements."

"True. Though he would find some interest in the company you've been keeping of late." He felt his master's gaze upon him.

For a moment, Scorpius doubted that he'd be able to hide his fear from Lord Thibault — fear for the safety of someone who might as well be his brother. He forced himself to glance over as he said, "Suppose the duke heard a report. What then?"

They reached the upper floor and passed by several servants and slaves, forcing his master to hold his tongue. Once they reached their rooms and began peeling away sweat-soaked tunics and breeches, his master looked up with eyes twinkling.

"You know, I've found myself dreaming of just that," Lord Thibault said. "Watching his face as I told him."

"Well?" Scorpius prodded. "What would happen, my lord? Was she not an invited guest?"

His master gazed off, his brow furrowed. Leading the way to the bath, he stepped in first and Scorpius followed, sighing as the warm water soothed tired muscles.

"We'll go riding this afternoon," Lord Thibault announced.

He gazed at Scorpius with promised answers lurking behind his eyes.

"As you wish, my lord." Scorpius eased back against the smooth stone, picturing his master's forbidden lover and her striped hair unfurling from her scarf. What sort of people could carry such markings? They seemed so fierce, and yet the chancellor with his hidden allegiance to the same people carried himself with calm reserve.

Why were they enemies of his lord's house? It must have taken a great deal of work before the chancellor infiltrated the duke's inner circle. Would Scorpius pay one day for stumbling onto this knowledge?

He gazed over at the slave washing Lord Thibault's shoulders. Did the slave ever worry about such things? Would Scorpius have had to wash his master if Richolf had not come for him, to raise him as a falconer's apprentice?

How bad could that be, really? Washing lords and fetching and tidying, pressing wrinkles from tunics and polishing jewelry. This slave ate, didn't he? He had a bed. Clothes to cover him.

What had Scorpius' life come to if he dreamed of the joys of slavery?

80

"I forget sometimes," his master said. "It seems odd you should be unaware of certain things."

They'd ridden hard over rough terrain. Both Lord Thibault and Scorpius worked to catch their breath as their mounts walked off the exertion.

"Do you mean to say that not even the chancellor has let you in on the rather more sensitive aspects of our glorious house?"

"He's told me some things, my lord." In truth, Scorpius could count on one hand the number of things about which the chancellor had informed him, but no matter.

"You've never spoken about the Sibiu?"

Scorpius looked closely at his master. Lord Thibault showed no sign that he concealed knowledge of their own chancellor belonging to such a fierce yet captivating people. Scorpius had played enough sessions at the gaming boards with Lord Thibault to know each one of his master's tells.

"And I suppose you didn't have much contact with them, out at the falconer's cottage," Lord Thibault said.

"Only at the estate when I went to trade in the pelts, my lord. Where do their lands lie?"

"No one recalls." His master sent him a look that Scorpius found puzzling. Lord Thibault's air of perpetual bemusement had dimmed since the ball which his mother, the dukessa had thrown for him and his prospective brides.

It reminded Scorpius of that moment out on the hunting field several years earlier, just before the attempt on the young noble's life. Lord Thibault had dropped his air of jovial entitlement to reveal a knife-edged sense of purpose, as well as a willingness to cross barriers of rank without blinking.

"The Sibiu are a people who live everywhere and nowhere."

When he offered nothing further, Scorpius thought back to the jewels and gold, even coins worn as adornment by these people with no homeland. "They would not be welcomed easily into a noble house such as yours, my lord."

Instead of the wry laugh he was expecting, Scorpius was pinned once more by a glance from his master, laden with dangerous longing.

For her.

"We must be clear, Scorpius. We can never speak of her. Not where even one ear could hear us."

Bowing forward in the saddle, Scorpius said, "Yes, my lord."

Lord Thibault looked up and toward the west, until he spied something. Nodding to himself, his master reached into his doublet and withdrew a thin scroll tied up in a leather sleeve.

Reaching across to take it, a heavy warning dragged at Scorpius' heart.

"Do you see that pass in the hills, there?" his master said.

"Yes, my lord."

Raising his hand to the sun, Lord Thibault flicked his wrist back and forth until the broad metal cuff he wore glinted in a rhythmic pattern. It only took a few heart beats before an answering glint appeared along the shadowy pass in the distance.

"Deliver this to the man who will be waiting for you at the head of the pass."

Scorpius secreted the scroll inside a fold of his jerkin. His senses sharpened as he made ready to strike out for the meeting place, which his mount sensed. The animal raised its head and pricked its ears, tensing to be off.

"Whatever they say or do, you must not leave until he has given you an answer. Are we clear?" Lord Thibault's face was as grim as the morning before Scorpius was delivered to his master's uncle, as a prisoner.

"As you command, my lord." Digging in his heels, Scorpius rode off before the warning in his gut could overrule his obedience to his master.

81

As he neared the head of the pass, Scorpius leaned into the saddle and pressed with his leg to guide his mount, twisting slightly to scan for signs of the expected recipient of the message tucked into his jerkin. Scorpius' mixed signals stopped the horse in its tracks, nearly sending Scorpius tumbling head over heels.

Pulling himself upright in the saddle, he barely had a chance to register the hands grabbing him by the shoulders. Dragged backwards, the breath knocked out of him as he hit the ground hard, his empty lungs held his full attention.

Once they filled again, Scorpius hung in the grip of Sibian scouts, his mount pulling hard against his reins but stopped by one of their war band. That was all he saw.

Someone pulled a hood pulled roughly over his face, and he was bound and thrown over a saddle. Scorpius slipped dangerously close to falling off the mount without hands to grip anything, and the jostling made it hard to breathe with the hood and the pressure of his body weight. He didn't know if it was a relief when he felt hands hauling him roughly backwards.

His feet touched the ground but he couldn't stop himself from sprawling onto his back. The hood was whisked away and a man stepped forward to gaze imperiously down upon him.

"How did you know to look for us?" he said in a gravelly voice.

He took one moment to gather his wits, scanning the other faces who all gazed down at him. Scorpius felt that he mustn't speak from this prone position. Not among this lot.

In two quick motions, he rolled to his knees and sprang to his feet. The Sibiu surrounding him tensed as though making ready to fight, but the speaker smiled and laughed.

"Did you not call for me?" Scorpius said. He was glad he was taller than any of them.

The lead scout took two steps forward, closing the gap. He didn't seem at all cowed by being shorter than Scorpius. "You don't look like the one I was calling," the scout said.

"Do you suppose my lord comes when called?" Scorpius said, making certain to meet the gazes of all those surrounding him.

Several chuckles erupted from the men. The hair on the back of Scorpius' neck prickled.

"What does your master say then, messenger?"

"If you reach inside my clothes over my heart, you'll find a scroll."

The sharp gaze of the lead scout raked over Scorpius from head to foot. As though satisfying himself that it was worth the risk, he deftly reached into the fold beneath Scorpius' jerkin and found the scroll straightaway.

Untying the lace that held it together, the Sibian unrolled and read it, his gaze flicking up to threaten Scorpius as he did so.

What could he be warning him against? Scorpius couldn't fathom it. The men surrounded him, he was bound and he didn't know where he was. Still, if the Sibian felt he had to caution Scorpius not to consider attacking when he was outnumbered and without weapons, it only made Scorpius draw himself as tall as he could to look down upon them all.

82

"Why would your master suggest such a thing?" asked the leader of this group of Sibiu. He gave no hint as to his own feelings about the contents of the scroll. He merely held it before him, glancing from Scorpius to the message and back again.

Scorpius remembered what Lord Thibault had instructed before sending him to this rendezvous.

Whatever they say or do, you must not leave until he has given you an answer. Are we clear?

Scorpius fought to contain the dark chuckle that rose inside him.

"If you suppose my master would tell me what is meant for your eyes only, you don't understand the House of Pruzhnino," Scorpius said.

To his relief, the lead Sibian nodded to one of the others who joined him for a measured conversation in their language. Taking care not to fidget as his heightened state demanded, Scorpius instead stood unmoving, hoping to appear unfazed though he was surrounded by fierce fighting men.

Since his hands were behind his back and out of sight, he allowed himself the luxury of twisting the dukessa's dragon ring back and forth on his finger. It kept him focused, and the connection to the estate gave him the courage he needed.

It was nearly impossible to stop himself from backing up a step as the leader approached with a menacing stride. He met the man's gaze and hoped his rising alarm stayed hidden in the recesses of his pounding heart.

"Your master insults us with his suggestion," the Sibian said, spitting at Scorpius' feet.

His stomach felt like a great weight dropped from a bridge. Drawing himself as tall as he could, he said, "My master honors you with an offer. At considerable risk to his noble house. If my hands were not tied, I would call you out."

A little gleam of respect flickered through the older man's

gaze, though his daunting expression remained. "You think you are a match for me?" the Sibian said, and the men laughed. "And after me, all of them?" He stepped back, gesturing to the band of men, all of whom sported scars.

"My master sent me, didn't he?" Scorpius said, shrugging as though taking on six men would be merely a training exercise. In order to gauge his chances if this escalated, Scorpius silently planned which ones he would take down first if it came to that.

To Scorpius' shock, the Sibian leader's posture deflated slightly. Exchanging glances with the man with whom he'd discussed the contents of the scroll, the leader raised the message and said, "We have our own ways of dealing with this, as we have done since before the stories were passed down. Why should your master, or any of you, care about our herd so suddenly?"

Scorpius blinked. Herd? What herd?

Think.

These people who lived everywhere and nowhere somehow maintained herds. The duke's estate — and every estate Scorpius had visited — displayed sweeping herds that enriched their holdings.

Once again Scorpius had to fight to hold back a laugh. If he had to take on six fighters over a thing like grazers, his master would live to regret it.

83

Scorpius squeezed the dukessa's dragon ring once more for courage.

Then an idea struck.

"I cannot speak for my master," Scorpius said to the leader. "I can only speak for myself. If you will retrieve my ring, I'll leave it with you as ransom for the proposal set forth by my master. When your business with him is done, I will retrieve it. If you agree."

The leader looked again to his trusted aide. At a signal between them, the aide broke away and closed the distance between himself and Scorpius.

Straightening his hand as best he could in the circumstances, Scorpius felt the Sibian take hold of the ring and pull. A surprising sense of loss coursed through him

As though the Sibian felt it, too, the fighter gasped as if he'd been run through with a blade. For a breathless moment, Scorpius was certain they all could hear the way his heart pounded.

The aide backed away from him, holding the ring as though it were made of jagged glass. He crossed the clearing to present the ring to their leader, who took hold of it with wary fascination.

In a hushed tone, he spoke a single word in the Sibian language.

The band of fighters repeated his whispered word, shrinking back from Scorpius as though licked by fire.

What was going on? He fought for breath, hands straining against the bonds behind his back.

The leader and his aide bent their heads together in frantic debate. Scorpius watched as the rest of the band grew pale, their haunted gazes raking him with dread.

When the aide bolted away into the shadows, Scorpius felt the undercurrent of alarm among the men rise even higher. His fingers reflexively reached for the ring he'd just offered as surety.

Grumpy bleating and tingling bells announced the arrival

of a modest herd of animals. The aide drove them through the pass to an open ridge. As he moved the animals into position, the lead Sibian approached his men, holding the ring high.

In a grave tone, he spoke to them in their own tongue. Scorpius saw the men bow their heads, all save one, who looked directly at him. Using every scrap of courage he possessed, Scorpius met this man's gaze.

The Sibian looked back at the ring, then up at the sky as though listening for the *whoosh* of those leathery wings. Then he bowed deeply before the leader, touching his lips to the ring before heading to the ridge to stand among the herd.

The aide passed him on his way back to join the others. He stopped and they embraced for a long moment.

When the aide's knife plunged into the other man's back, Scorpius' blood ran cold.

84

Whipping around to keep his sights on the rest of the Sibiu, Scorpius prepared himself for a fight.

He found only men standing with bowed heads, their lips moving in prayer.

Looking back to see the aide pulling his knife free of his kinsman's back, Scorpius' heart raced as he made ready to flee. Yet the Sibiu weren't as distracted as he'd hoped.

Strong hands took hold of his bound arms and held him in place. He knew it was useless to struggle, but he couldn't stop himself from wrestling against their grip.

The man who'd been stabbed started to sag slightly in the arms of the aide. Perhaps sensing the suffering of the one in their midst, the animals in the herd shifted and bleated uneasily.

Adding to the sense that the very ground beneath Scorpius' feet had turned to sand, an eerie tune filtered skyward. Craning his neck to stare, Scorpius saw several of the Sibiu blowing into carved wooden pipe instruments. The hair on the back of his neck rose at the sound of the music, at the cries of the herd and the gasping of the stabbed man.

Dragging him so that Scorpius stumbled backward, the Sibiu forced him down onto his face, pressed close to the sheer rock of the mountain pass. Joining him as near as they could, the Sibiu who held him fast ducked their heads low and continued to pray.

At first it was so distant, he thought he imagined it.

A thing to haunt one's dreams, as it had done for most of his life. Ever since that horrifying day when he still lived at the nursery, the day his little friend had not rolled quickly enough under the hole in the fence. The smell of her burning flesh, her screech of agony, the sound of the leathery wings gliding over the top of him had never left him.

When Richolf had come for him, when he was still a young boy, it had flown overhead as he'd tried to make his way to the Pillar Rock. His former master had rolled him beneath a rock ledge just as these Sibiu were doing now.

Over the rising din of the animals, which scattered and ran in circles as they failed to find a route off the ridge, Scorpius heard it now. The Sibiu kept playing their pipes and praying, but the sickening sound of the enormous wings seized hold of him, leaving him frozen with dread.

Scorpius would have given anything — anything — to be spared the sight and sound and smell of this. Trembling with fear, he could only watch as the aide kissed the dying man's forehead, then broke their embrace and ran as fast as anyone Scorpius had ever seen. The herd ran frantically with him, their eyes white with terror.

The dragon swooped low, its size and speed too great for those on the ground. Diving to the edge of the ridge, the running Sibian disappeared from view just as the man he'd left behind finally sagged in a heap upon the smooth rock.

An intense blast of heat lit the mountain pass. Wind raced ahead of the dragon's fire, whipping Scorpius' hair into his eyes, stealing the breath from his lungs.

The piped music, the bleating, the praying, the scream of the stabbed Sibian all fell away under the deafening roar from that scaly throat.

85

It was difficult but not impossible to ride, considering the horse was as determined as Scorpius to leave the Sibiu behind. They'd left him the saddle, at least, which he grabbed with his bound hands wrenched fast behind his back. Leaning as far forward as he could without losing his grip, Scorpius hugged the horse with his legs, trusting it to pick its own way back out of the pass.

They raced against the lengthening shadows with the stink of scorched flesh clinging fast. Hoof beats drummed in time to Scorpius' heart, filling his mind as he strained to listen for the rhythmic flapping of leathery wings.

Fighting the panic that stole the breath from him, Scorpius stared straight ahead but saw nothing except the horrible memory of the Sibian herd in his mind's eye, blooms of flame rolling forth from the shrieking mouth of the dragon. He and the horse were both intent on barreling past his master when he emerged at a run toward them.

"Whoa!" Lord Thibault said, waving his arms in broad circles.

The horse halted, sending Scorpius to slide abruptly forward. Jagged pain greeted his landing as he tumbled onto the rocky ground. His master jogged to grab the horse's mane, coaxing it to put aside its mindless flight for the time being.

Groaning, Scorpius struggled to his feet. Straining to see if the nightmare had followed them, he scanned the horizon but found it to be made of only sunset hues. The mountain pass gaped black and still, like a lie.

"Did you bring the message?" Lord Thibault asked.

"No message," Scorpius said, working to catch his breath.

The look of sickened disbelief that washed over his master reached into Scorpius' heart, still numbed by fear. Taking a few steps to close the gap between them, Scorpius kept his voice low so as not to distress the horse any further.

"No scroll, I meant to say, my lord."

"News, then?"

"Did you not see?" Scorpius said, hearing the stricken edge to his own voice.

"Of course I saw," Lord Thibault whispered.

Pulling himself as straight as he could, Scorpius fought to keep a normal tone to his voice. He grasped at this semblance of normalcy as though it could protect him like a charm.

He told of the Sibian's reaction to the scroll's suggestion, until Scorpius had offered his dragon ring in order to vouch for his master's word. Lord Thibault grabbed hold of him then and spun him around.

Scorpius' body jerked as his master sliced through the rope pinning his arms back.

"You gave them my mother's ring?" said his master.

Turning to face Lord Thibault, Scorpius said, "I did, my lord." He watched in fascination as his master flushed red.

"You shame me, Scorpius."

"My lord?"

"You forced their hand with that offer. I assume then that they refused my first one?"

"They did, my lord."

"Still, the herd was cleansed."

"The herd? The herd was burnt to a crisp!"

Stretching a hand out to clap it on Scorpius' shoulder, Lord Thibault smiled grimly. "The herd was ill. A herd which they hide amongst our own in order to graze them. There was much at stake."

Nodding, Scorpius gazed once more upon his master's red face, dust-worn doublet and the worn lines around his master's eyes — so deep for such a young man. The news he craved hadn't been passed to Scorpius in a scroll. A few words and Lord Thibault would have his answer.

"My lord," Scorpius said. "My lord, there's something you must know."

86

With trembling fingers, Scorpius reached inside his jerkin to retrieve a piece of patterned cloth. He gave it to Lord Thibault, who saw the shaking and placed his hand upon Scorpius' for a moment, to steady him.

Scorpius looked into his master's eyes to see disbelief rising close to the surface of hope. With a rough squeeze, his master released his hand. "I did tell you not to leave the Sibiu unless you'd secured an answer."

Nodding wearily, Scorpius said, "You did, my lord."

Lord Thibault squeezed the scrap of Sibian cloth as though it held him upright. "Of course, I may have left out the caveat concerning dragons."

"That's not all you failed to mention." A burst of anger rose in Scorpius' chest, forcing him to turn away from his master.

Closing the distance between them, Lord Thibault stood in silence until Scorpius' skin crawled. Still, he could not force himself to speak, to say words he did not mean.

"You remember what I told you that morning, before we sought shelter with my uncle," his master said.

"I remember it all, my lord."

"Is it now the duty of a duke's son to beg the pardon of his servant?"

Burning anger turned quickly to a sickening chill in the pit of his stomach. Still, Scorpius could not make himself speak.

"It has ever fallen to nobles to send men to their deaths, if need be," Lord Thibault said. "To ask them to suffer, even when they don't understand what they're suffering for."

"You've claimed your birthright, then." Scorpius half turned, but could not face Lord Thibault. Not if he wanted to spare his master the shock of a fist to the jaw.

"Dashed it to pieces, you mean." His master circled around to stand before him. He held up the wrinkled cloth for both of them to see. "You have brought me the keys to the destruction of the House of Pruzhnino. If I had told you this, would you have delivered the scroll to the Sibiu?"

87

The chill that squeezed Scorpius' guts splintered into icy clarity.

Before he dared let reason intrude, Scorpius burst forward to charge his master, taking him down in a breath-stealing crash. Too late, Lord Thibault fought to hang onto the message sent from the envoy in the secret mountain pass, the message formed by Sibian patterns in a dusty scrap of cloth.

Scorpius had been bound, blindfolded, delivered to the Sibiu, charged with delivering a message whose contents he had not known and ordered not to return without an answer. He'd been thrown to the ground, threatened by men and blistered by the heat of the gliding leathery monster of his nightmares. If the telltale patterned scrap of cloth sent by the Sibian commander threatened the security of his master's house, well, something snapped inside of Scorpius.

A sharp blow from his elbow numbed Lord Thibault's fingers. Scorpius peeled the cloth free from his master's grip, but Lord Thibault would not give up so easily.

Hurling himself in a roll forward, his master grabbed Scorpius' legs to prevent his escape. Scorpius grunted as his chin hit the ground, but he kept hold of the scrap of cloth.

A flashing glance showed the same expression any adversary of Lord Thibault would see, just before the killing stroke slipped between unsuspecting ribs.

As cleanly as his former falcon master Richolf's red tail hawk took down a game hen, Scorpius butted heads with his master, knocking Lord Thibault off balance just long enough for Scorpius to swipe the small dagger from its place at his hip.

Recovering, his master kicked up to wrap his legs around Scorpius' hips, rolling him. There was no keeping hold of both the cloth and the dagger. As Scorpius' face ground into the dirt, he loosened his grip on the cloth but tightened his fingers around the dagger hilt.

With all of his might, Scorpius tried to push the momentum

farther than his master intended, but Lord Thibault had trained with the same sword master as he. For a crushing moment, Scorpius was immobilized.

Both of them panted for breath.

He knew his master would reach for the cloth. All he had to do was wait.

At the split second when he felt Lord Thibault's weight shift, Scorpius made his move. Twisting hard to face up towards his master, Scorpius forced Lord Thibault's attention away from the cloth. Planting his feet solidly against the ground, Scorpius bucked hard with his legs, pitching his master forward.

A mad scramble scattered dust and pebbles along with limbs, fists and feet. Scorpius dug in hard, pinning Lord Thibault's head in a chokehold with his legs, locking one of his master's arms awkwardly to the side. With his other hand he slid the dagger within a hair's- breadth of his master's eye.

Lord Thibault stilled. "This is a death sentence," he said.

Scorpius chuckled. "Bringing down your noble house would end in the same way for you."

"I didn't say I wanted to bring it down."

"You said the cloth made way for the fall of the House of Pruzhnino."

"I didn't say that's what I wanted," his master said, his voice tight with pain.

"You don't say it because I have a dagger in place to put out your eye."

"Why should you care?" Lord Thibault's voice rose with unaccustomed passion. "What possible difference does the Pruzhnino line make to you?"

"You ask that of me? Me, with no father. No mother. Me, who only ever had Richolf, and you sent even him from me."

"And yet you have served me. All these years, you have served me."

"Do you think someone like me has a choice?" Scorpius fought the rage that wanted to set him shaking. He concentrated on keeping the dagger tip still as Lord Thibault's lashes blinked against it.

"What do you think that cloth represents?" his master said, pulling his gaze away from the blade to look deeply into Scorpius' eyes. "That cloth is my choice. And she said yes."

88

Scorpius fought the urge to look back into his memories, needing every part of him to remain here in this moment. Pressing his master firmly into the dirt, Scorpius kept his dagger blade trained a mere whisper away from Lord Thibault's eye.

"So the lord exercises his right to choose," Scorpius said between clenched teeth, admitting for the first time how wide the chasm between them truly stretched.

"That's right. I refuse every excuse for a bride they've been parading before me."

He couldn't help it. Scorpius' mind cast back to the last time he'd seen his master with the Sibian maiden, clutching her to him, pulling sighs from her lips.

That was all it took, one split second of distraction and Lord Thibault made his move. Scorpius' dagger spun from his hand. His master rolled forward, crushing Scorpius' neck and shoulders into the ground. The motion wrenched Lord Thibault's arm, ripping a cry from him but failing to block his escape.

Scorpius scrambled to retain a hold upon his master, but found himself pinned instead. The blood in his veins shot through with icy dread.

This is a death sentence, his master had said.

Lord Thibault's rigid fingers pressed like darts into Scorpius' throat.

Working to catch his breath, his master said, "After everything we have been through. You would fight to stop me in this."

Scorpius fought to read the emotion in Lord Thibault's eyes. A lifetime of training cloaked his master's heart from revealing itself.

Words could not form with Lord Thibault's fingers choking him. Still, he forced his lips to move, his breath to rasp out whatever it could.

"Why bring down your noble house?" he said.

"You fight even me to protect my family?" Lord Thibault said.

"Can you not simply flee?" Scorpius said. "You seek union with her. Can they not take you to live among them?"

After a long moment, his master eased off the pressure on Scorpius' throat, still keeping him firmly pinned. "If I had done that, would you have followed me there?"

A flare of anger filled Scorpius with reckless disregard for self-preservation. "You forget that I've never had the luxury of choice, my lord."

He was unprepared for the emotion that flooded his master's face. "So you would have elected to stay in my father's house."

"How do I know what I might have chosen? You did not give me such a gift."

Abruptly, Lord Thibault pushed up from the hold he'd used to immobilize Scorpius. Gazing down as he fought to conceal the myriad of feelings that battled within him, his master said, "No, I did not. Instead I have an attempt on my life."

Pacing in agitation, Lord Thibault halted in his tracks. "We will return to the palace," he said, stooping to pick up the scrap of Sibian cloth. "If any word of this circulates, I will know its source. At which time, my memory of your dagger drawn against me will surface."

Scorpius regained his feet. "Understood, my lord."

"I don't think I understand *you*, Scorpius. If you only knew who it was that the Chancellor suspects of siring you. If you did, you would not be so quick to defend my father, the duke. You would be just as eager as I to leave them all behind."

89

Riders met them on the approach to the long road that led through the estate. There was nothing for it but to coax their mounts forward, surrounded by the duke's men. The disapproval of his master's father dimmed the cheer of the sunny afternoon, preventing even Lord Thibault from mustering his customary grin.

By the time they'd dismounted to enter the echoing corridors, Scorpius wondered if he was in fact being delivered to the duke for judgment. The fact that Lord Thibault was hemmed in by guards alongside him certainly confused the issue.

How would anyone here know what had happened between his master and himself, anyway? Yet the guards flanked them forward and back, on the left side and the right.

They all turned the corner heading for the duke's drawing room, every man pulling himself a little taller, taking a breath for courage before crossing the threshold.

Fanning out across the back of the room, the guard halted as Lord Thibault and Scorpius stepped forward. Together they bowed, Scorpius bending lower in a reverence. Two of the guard placed the swords they'd confiscated upon the duke's desk and backed away as Lord Thibault's father rose to his feet.

The chancellor stepped out of the shadows to round the enormous desk as though clearing the way for his master, the duke. Scorpius raised his eyes to lock gazes for a brief moment with the chancellor, whose grim expression did nothing for the sinking feeling in Scorpius' gut.

Black boots polished to an impossible shine came to a stop before Lord Thibault.

A crisp gesture from the chancellor sent the guard turning on its heel to file out through the golden double doors. Only when the click of the door handle drenched the room in heavy silence did Lord Thibault straighten.

His Grace the Duke of Pruzhnino swung a jeweled hand. Scorpius' master sprawled on the patterned carpet, his shocked grunt hanging in the air.

"I don't need to tell you there was a dragon sighting," the duke said. "Do I?"

Lord Thibault touched the back of his hand to his bleeding lip. "I was aware of it."

"Were you planning to inform me as to what it was you were doing in the very path of that thing?"

"Not really."

Scorpius saw the glint of fury light the duke's eyes a split second before he swung again. As though time had somehow slowed, Scorpius flung himself down in time to cover his master's body with his own. The duke's powerful blow drew a cry from Scorpius but did not dislodge him.

Only the wrenching yank of the duke's hand grabbing his hair managed that.

Scorpius was dragged to his knees. Fighting the urge to grab the duke's hand in order to take some of the pressure from his scalp, Scorpius raised himself as tall as he could but it did no good. A few sharp shakes from the duke and dizziness clouded his vision.

"Please, Papa!" Lord Thibault called, a note of real fear exposing itself in his voice. "My man seeks only to protect me."

"He did a piss poor job of it."

"I beg Your Grace's forgiveness," Scorpius said.

"You do not have it," the duke growled, shoving Scorpius forward.

"Well, he has mine, and he's my man." Lord Thibault regained his feet, shaking off the last few moments as though none of it had happened. Shooting a glance down at Scorpius, he flicked his head up as if to say that Scorpius should join him.

"You were consorting with the Sibiu," the duke said, taking a few strides away from his son, stopping to turn. The look that promised retribution on his face turned Scorpius' insides to jelly.

90

"I don't expect you to understand, Father," Lord Thibault said as Scorpius rose to his feet. "Though how can it be so — that I should be the only one to have considered such a course of action?"

Scorpius braced himself for the duke to lash out once more at his son's impudence. Strangely, Lord Thibault's boldness seemed to soothe his father, who crossed his arms and said, "Go on."

"The fables that warn of the Sibiu's ability to call forth the dragon are not stories, Father." Extending his arm to indicate Scorpius, Lord Thibault locked gazes with him for a suspended moment. The master who could meet anything with a cavalier grin had only resolute warning in his eyes. "My man is a witness to it."

Blinking back the dread that stopped his tongue, Scorpius squared his shoulders and held his ground as Pruzhnino turned his attention to him.

Forcing himself to speak in a measured voice, Scorpius explained all he had seen in the hidden mountain pass. He told the duke about the rejected offer from his master until Scorpius used the dukessa's dragon ring as surety. He described the sacrificial stabbing of the Sibian, the praying of the men, the eerie playing of the pipes until the great dragon itself appeared in the air above them.

A withering gaze from the duke raked Scorpius from head to foot before Pruzhnino turned back to his son and said, "The Sibiu still have your mother's ring in their possession?"

Bowing slightly, Lord Thibault said, "They do, Your Grace."

The duke was so quick, his master gasped to find himself half-lifted off his feet, the neck of his doublet in his father's iron fists. Before he could stop himself, Scorpius' hand flew to his hip, where his sword no longer hung. Thank the gods no one but the chancellor had seen what amounted to an attempt on the life of Pruzhnino.

Gazing over in fear at the chancellor, Scorpius was met by a gaze dark with grim reassurance.

"They will trace that ring to this house," the duke said.

"Let them," Lord Thibault said.

"I will do no such thing." Shaking his son before shoving him away, the duke moved to join the chancellor.

Recovering his balance, Lord Thibault drew himself up and once again carried on his conversation as though nothing was amiss. "The stories are not stories, Father. We have amongst us a means of drawing forth the thing which every dominion in every land fears above all else."

The duke and the chancellor turned to give Scorpius' young master their full attention. The air crackled with all that was forbidden.

"It was my man's idea to give them the ring. I'd forgotten that it bore a dragon upon it. They took it as a sign, and thank the gods they did. Otherwise they might never have called what cannot be called."

"And what should that mean to me?" the duke said. "Other than to draw up a plan to retrieve your mother's ring before word reaches any other house that it's in Sibian hands?"

Once again the duke raked his gaze over Scorpius like a swipe from a claw. Scorpius' heart pounded in his chest. Did his master know what he was doing?

If this all blew up in his master's face, where would that leave him? The rage at being at the mercy of these struggles for dominance, at having his fate decided by whichever set of nobles held the winning hand, pushed down the fear that threatened to choke him.

He remembered the look on his master's face as they fought in the mountains. *You forget that I've never had the luxury of choice, my lord*, Scorpius had said.

Lord Thibault stared down his father the duke and his chancellor. What choices did his master have, other than to obey his father's will and that of his house?

Still, Scorpius calculated how far he'd have to dive to retrieve the swords from the duke's desk, if it came to that.

91

"You asked me to choose a bride," Lord Thibault said. The tension in the duke's drawing room tightened like a wire noose embedding itself into Scorpius' neck.

"Well, I have chosen her. She comes with a dowry of gold and jewels, but no land. Her people will deliver to the House of Pruzhnino a sceptre of power unparalleled among the dominions."

The fervor burning in his master's eyes held them all in its hypnotic sway. "Our house will be held highest in the annals of glory as the first of any generation to control the dragon."

After a tomb-like silence, during which Scorpius was certain the duke could hear his nervous swallowing, Pruzhnino uncrossed his arms and made his way over the patterned carpet to stand before his son.

"Do they know of this choice of yours?" he said, so casually it made the hair on Scorpius' neck stand on end.

Lord Thibault drew himself up tall before his father, only the clenching of his jaw giving himself away. "I am your son, Your Grace," he said, inclining his head warily. "I seek permission to join this house with another."

When his words failed to provoke a blow, Scorpius' master raised his head to meet his father's gaze. "It's true — I beg you to consider that which has never before been attempted. And yet, Father, I would have this union arranged in accordance with our customs."

Scorpius' heart seized tight in his chest as the Pruzhnino's expression darkened. The ornate drawing room seemed only a heartbeat away from igniting in the shrieking flames of that mountain pass, among the Sibiu.

"There is a reason that no other noble house has attempted a union with the Sibiu," the chancellor said in his calming tone.

Unable to stop himself from glancing at the man who'd revealed to Scorpius his secret Sibian heritage, Scorpius saw that the chancellor had taken note of Scorpius' attempts to sidle unnoticed closer and closer to the confiscated swords atop the duke's desk.

"A formal one, you mean," Pruzhnino said. "There isn't one noble line without its Sibian bastard."

Scorpius forced himself to stare at the floor. If the duke or his master were to discover their chancellor was one of these bastards because of any clue Scorpius gave away, he would never forgive himself.

"Yes, and that reason is fast becoming pointless, Father," Lord Thibault said. "We bury ourselves further and further into The Troubles, and no one has ever found a way out of it. Well, if our houses fall, the Sibiu fall with us. Yashtii's people agree with me. Let it be our house that leads the way out of the mess we're in."

Scorpius held his breath as a timepiece *tick, ticked* in the heavy afternoon.

92

"Yashtii's people," the duke repeated. "You think to align the House of Pruzhnino with a girl whose 'people' hide in mountain passes?"

Lord Thibault crossed his arms before him. "And which bride did you have picked out for me, Father?"

"That little golden-haired morsel sent by Razlava," the duke said. "You were not averse to her charms, by all accounts. And she brings a much-needed ally from the north."

Scorpius' master gazed down at the carpet for a long moment. Holding his position, still several paces away from their confiscated swords, Scorpius locked gazes with the chancellor. With his own secret to hide, the duke's advisor — whose Sibian hair markings remained concealed beneath his hat — kept his eye on Scorpius' attempts to reclaim his weapon while choosing not to alert the duke.

"A northern ally will not make one speck of difference to The Troubles." Lord Thibault looked up at his father, his eyes once again lit with an internal fire. "Yashtii's people can call forth the most destructive force in the twelve dominions combined. If we could hold that terror over the heads of the other houses, The Troubles would cease."

"If all it took to end The Troubles was the dragon, the Sibiu would have called one forth, generations past," the chancellor said.

"How do we know they didn't, Your Grace?" Scorpius said. "Perhaps no one ever bothered to connect the sightings with alliances and clashes between the houses."

All heads turned to regard him. Scorpius swallowed.

"Every sighting is recorded," the chancellor said.

"By ourselves and the Sibiu, both," Lord Thibault said with excitement coloring his cheeks. "Imagine what we could accomplish if it could be shown that we have the power to aim the stuff of nightmares into the hearts of our enemies' strongholds?"

"You sound bewitched, boy," the duke said.

Instead of taking offense, as Scorpius had been certain his master would do, Lord Thibault grinned widely. "I am, Father. As will you be."

"You are my second son, Thibault, and with the possibility that my heir, the markiisi, might one day come to harm, you must marry as if it were you and not your brother who is marked to ascend to the dukedom."

"Of course, Father."

"An alliance with a hidden people who lurk amongst us, concealing their flocks among ours, using our resources but shouldering none of the costs — this kind of alliance will weaken ties between the House of Pruzhnino and many other families."

"The Troubles have kept every tie between us and the other families so stretched that many have snapped of their own accord. Why not try a new way? The old way has brought nothing but distrust and destruction."

The duke stood gazing at his son for a long, long moment.

"You will announce an intimate soiree, Thibault," the duke said at last. "Invite a handful from the fête. You will include the golden-haired northerner, and you may invite your Sibian candidate. I will take another look at this girl."

Lord Thibault's father started to turn back towards his desk, when his son flung himself to one knee and grabbed the duke's hand in his own.

Kissing his father's ring, Lord Thibault's smile filled the drawing room with his joy.

93

The chancellor joined him as Scorpius leaned forward over the gallery railings, overlooking the guests already swirling in patterns to the music. While his master met privately with the duke and dukessa, now was as good a time as any to get the feel of the room.

Without drawing attention by performing the crisp movements of a proper reverence, Scorpius straightened, nodding in an approximation of respectful greeting. Feeling the chancellor's smile more than seeing it, Scorpius said, "My Lord Chancellor."

"My lord's man." The chancellor stood silently beside him for a time before saying, "And what do you make of this night's prospects?"

"All seems to be as it should. Which will only keep me looking more sharply for that which lies hidden."

"You would make a good chancellor one day, Scorpius. Once your fighting days are past." Turning to lean against the railing with his back to the guests, the chancellor imperceptibly positioned his arm to reveal a knotted scar running across his wrist.

"And how did my Lord Chancellor come to this service?" Scorpius asked, staring out at the dancers. "It's not something to which one is apprenticed, surely. Not like a falconer who needs a boy."

"We in this service need to find someone who can learn what is impossible to teach. Unlike your old master, we cannot simply get ourselves to the nursery and arrange for an unclaimed bastard to begin training."

Scorpius' mouth opened in shock before he could get hold of the pain erupting in his heart. He felt the loss of Richolf as though he'd only just ridden away from him in the blackness of the night woods. A breathtaking crush inside his gut slammed into him as he remembered the day Richolf had appeared at the nursery, not as a member of the family he'd never known, but as a master sporting marks warning of what lay in wait for a life lived amongst birds of prey.

Taking a calming breath, Scorpius moved back a pace, making eye contact with the chancellor. "Who taught you all that could not be taught?"

The chancellor seemed to look inward for a long moment. "A man who could have revealed something, but did not." He gazed at Scorpius as the memory of that morning in the stables, when the chancellor had revealed his Sibian-patterned hair, passed between them.

"I promised you then that the young woman from the northern house was waiting upon her grandsire to fetch her back, or to make arrangements here if she was found suitable. Her family will be arriving at the soiree shortly."

Scorpius' heart beat erratically. Why was the chancellor telling him about that fair-haired beauty? It was all he could do to stand there when he wanted to run out of here, run and run until he was too out of breath to notice anything but his lungs burning for air.

Forcing himself to turn towards the chancellor, Scorpius was just in time to catch the silhouette of the duke's minister nodding to Lord Thibault as he slipped into the crowd. A satisfied grin spread across his master's face as he swept Scorpius along the gallery, heading for the stairs.

"It's all set," Lord Thibault said, boots clicking impatiently on the polished flagstone.

"Good news, then," Scorpius said, keeping pace with his master, one hand gripping the pommel of his sword at his hip.

"The best. The very best." As they neared the first corner, the privacy of the upper gallery gave way to guests who stopped and bowed to Lord Thibault. "And not only for me, though the gods only know why." Again he shot Scorpius a grin.

It nearly made him catch his feet in a stumble. "My lord?" he asked.

"Tonight I am permitted to flirt to my heart's content with the charming northern lady whom my family apparently have chosen for me. I am also permitted to flirt with Yashtii, whom

I love. Isn't that rich?"

They began to make their way down the stairs, pressing through the crowd. Scorpius forced himself to keep his gaze on possible dangers as his lord's man must do.

"Tonight I am permitted to choose my bride. No matter that my heart is already given to my adored Sibian maiden, apparently I'm still to choose between Yashtii and the northerner. Don't you know what this means, Scorpius?"

Lord Thibault stopped in his tracks. "It means that I have won a great battle. They have agreed to honor my choice."

Purpose glowed in his master's eyes. "My choice is to unite my house with the Sibiu."

Reaching forward, Lord Thibault grabbed Scorpius by the arms. "I haven't forgotten what you said in the mountain pass, Scorpius. About choice. About never having been given a choice."

Looking over his shoulder and down into the crowd below, Lord Thibault returned his gaze to Scorpius. "My choice tonight will only leave me wanting you beside me more than ever. You have a choice of your own to make."

The fear lurking behind his master's joy made Scorpius' stomach swirl with warning.

94

He looked at his master, bringing his own arms up to clasp Lord Thibault's. Time hung suspended as Scorpius' master's haunted gaze met his own. Soiree guests glided past them along the stairs, their movements seeming oddly slow to Scorpius, as though they moved through lake water.

Blood pounded in his ears as he turned to look behind him, over the stair railing down into the crowd below. He sought the Sibian woman who had won Lord Thibault's heart, setting them both hurtling into this night where they reached for the prize.

There she was, dazzling in her bold colors, glowing with gold coins and gleaming jewels. Only an arm's length away from Lord Thibault's love, the fair-haired northern maiden stood amongst friends and a family escort.

The chancellor's words rumbled through his mind: *The young lady whose approval has been given by the dukessa and myself is from a well-placed family to the north, whose grandsire will be arriving after the next moon to collect her. I will arrange for you to attend me when the duke calls an audience with her grandsire.*

All families have faces they show to the world, and faces they protect. Injured sides, shameful sides, monstrous sides. Some families have mysteries, never solved. Until someone uncovers just the right shape to solve the puzzle.

Scorpius looked again at his master, who just slightly nodded his head. A small gesture that shredded Scorpius' heart.

"If we were not here before all of these guests, Scorpius, I would kneel and beg your forgiveness."

Breath catching in his chest, Scorpius whispered, "My lord?" As if compelled to look, he glanced down at the fair-haired lady softly glowing in her delicate finery.

Lord Thibault squeezed his fingers tighter around Scorpius' arms. "I never thought to help you search out your family when I brought you here. I just wanted you for my man."

Scorpius bowed his head against the pain seizing up in his

chest. He tried to speak but nothing came out.

"I've been a selfish bastard," Lord Thibault said, releasing his hold on him.

"Please, don't," Scorpius said, shaking his head no.

"At least the chancellor has been a true friend to you. He followed the trail at once."

Turning to gaze out over the crowd, Scorpius whispered, "It cannot be safe to speak here."

"They all believe we would never do so, and are paying us no heed." Lord Thibault looked sideways at him, but where there should have been a grin was only shadow and pale self-reproach. "I am going to make my choice tonight. You are going to make yours. If it turns out that —"

His master's voice faltered. Lord Thibault angled his body away for a long moment.

"I have two brothers, Scorpius. Neither of whom knows my heart the way you do. I will always consider you my true brother. And I do beg your forgiveness."

"My lord," Scorpius said, his voice breaking.

"That's just it," Lord Thibault said, finally smiling. "You may be every bit a lord in your own right. All you have to do is attend upon the chancellor when her grandsire meets with my father the duke after the soiree. It will all be up to you, Scorpius. Make yourself known to the Duke of Razlava, with whom my father wishes to form an alliance.

"It is said he lost a daughter who made free with all the delights of the world. She tasted of these fruits until they were her only gods. Our chancellor discovered she'd left a child behind at the nursery, unable to stop herself from plucking as many pleasures from the world as she could before she died of all of it."

Scorpius' heart beat so hard he could barely hear his master anymore.

"Her father did not claim the boy-child. The origin of the baby's father was unverifiable, and therefore suspect. The north-erners are proud of their stock and unwelcoming to common bloodlines ruining their pedigrees."

Lord Thibault looked into Scorpius' eyes. "You are too dark to belong to their line. You were not claimed. And yet the lovely fair-haired one so favored by my mother is your cousin. If the chancellor swears to it, it is so."

95

They danced for hours, cutting figures and counting measures with sly twists, secret smiles and discreet brushes past the two maidens. Scorpius locked gazes with his master's intended, searching for answers in the swiftest of moments. Then the music swung them apart.

Yashtii, the Sibian maiden whose hold on his master had set The Troubles past the simmer point, ducked and swayed with abandon, the brimming passion in her movements unmatched by the graceful ladies surrounding her. Though she wove through the dances in the same assured manner as everyone here, Lord Thibault's intended inhabited the ballroom like no one else.

In fact, the fair-haired beauty — his cousin from the north whose name he did not even know — must have come to a conclusion regarding her prospects with his master. Though she'd begun the evening with a light step and a rather irresistible smile, as the night went on the glow left her face, her gazes falling before she could make eye contact with Lord Thibault.

The dancers snaked their way along the rows, joining hands and releasing, joining hands and releasing. Scorpius saw his cousin up ahead and determined he would catch her gaze, not sure what he would do once he had it, but unwilling to watch her sink into despair.

For a crushing moment he thought the dance might force them to miss one another, but another skip and a step and there she was. Yet it was she who sought Scorpius out, she whose gaze burned ahead before their hands reached out to grasp and hold.

He saw the hurt and confusion in her pale blue eyes, grayed over now with sadness. How it tugged at his heart, the way she looked up at him, deep into his eyes with a wordless demand for explanation. Spinning away on her pretty heel, Scorpius matched his cousin's speed in time to see her tip her head around to keep him in her sights.

His stomach swirled with unaccustomed exhilaration.

It seemed an age before the figures brought them around again. Scorpius nearly forgot to keep his habitual watch on the assembled guests even in the midst of his dancing. Darting a glance into the gallery, he saw the chancellor gazing down at him and imagined that the dark expression he saw there was an affirmation of Scorpius' neglect of duty.

Swinging his head around in time to the music, Scorpius found Lord Thibault exactly where he expected to find him along the promenade line. His master's hands were joined with Yashtii's, sparks bursting between them so that all were warmed by their joy.

When the set ended, Scorpius bowed to the lady across from him, then quickly turned and bowed to the northern maiden. Her blush brought him to her side, offering his arm and the promise of refreshment.

As though appearing from thin air, the fair-haired cousin's retinue of male kin bound them both on all sides. Scorpius did not break his stride, refusing to relinquish his position as lord's man to the host of the evening. "Enough for all, I dare say."

Her solidly-built kinsman stood firmly in the way. "She respectfully declines your kind offer, sir."

Releasing the lady's arm, Scorpius stepped back and bowed to the young fighter. "Lord's man, my lord." He straightened, making sure to avoid direct eye contact. "My master offers food and drink to rival any in the twelve dominions. Care to taste of its delicacies?"

"Perhaps your master's father, the duke may offer something better?" her kinsman said. "He has asked for you, my Lady Aerthrudha."

The fair-haired northern maiden looked back through the crowd towards Lord Thibault, only to hear his infectious laughter as he smiled at Yashtii. Pausing for only a moment, Lady Aerthrudha rejoined Scorpius, taking his arm and addressing the young fighter with disdain.

"Our host's man will no doubt know the way there," she said.

Bowing again, Scorpius turned them all in the direction

of the far staircase. "Come this way, if it would please my lords and my lady."

As they made their way up the stairs and along the corridor to the ornate doors leading to the duke's drawing room, the sounds of the soiree faded into the distance, until there was only the clicking of boots on the polished floor and the rich sweeping sounds of Lady Aerthrudha's gown.

Scorpius couldn't afford to let himself hear the pounding of his own pulse in his ears. Slaves pulled the doors open, Scorpius stepped forward with his unsuspecting cousin on his arm while her kinsman fanned out along the back of the drawing room.

The chancellor emerged from the shadows, catching Scorpius' gaze one second before a regal man turned from conversation with the Duke of Pruzhnino. The guest held his hands out to Lady Aerthrudha, who moved forward and clasped them warmly.

The blood in Scorpius' veins chilled as his breath caught. The lady's grandsire was no stranger.

Those hands had once yanked the folded leather from the young guard's mouth, so this noble could better hear his shrieks. Her grandsire, the Duke of Razlava, had once gone by the title of lord.

Lord Dirske. The architect of the Nightmare Hunt, the Hunt of Screams.

96

"My darling girl," Razlava said, kissing her forehead.

"Grandfather," she said, her voice tight with unshed tears.

"I do hope you have enjoyed your stay here," Pruzhnino said in a tone Scorpius had never heard coming from Lord Thibault's father before.

Lady Aerthrudha released her grandsire's hands and curtseyed deeply before the duke. "A peek inside the heavens could not have been sweeter."

"My dear," Lord Thibault's father said, bending to sweep the lady's fingers up to his lips, "my house will be the poorer for the loss of such a luminous guest as yourself."

Scorpius stood seeing and hearing, yet none of it seemed to make its way past the memories which swarmed foremost in his mind. He saw the image of the pale slave girl tiring of being run down in the hunting field, finally turning to meet her fate at the hands of Lord Dirske. Now Duke of Razlava.

Someone joined him, brushing beside him as if to hold him up.

"Remember what I told you," the chancellor said.

Scorpius glanced sideways. The duke's advisor wore a grim expression, yet he nodded and flicked his head forward as if to coax Scorpius toward the nobles.

You may be every bit a lord in your own right, his master had said on the stairs. *It will all be up to you, Scorpius. Make yourself known to the Duke of Razlava, with whom my father wishes to form an alliance.*

Scorpius shook his head, *no*.

"We can yet secure an alliance with this house if they claim you," the chancellor whispered.

"No!" Scorpius whispered hotly, as both dukes and the lady turned to regard him.

"Problem, my Lord Chancellor?" Razlava said.

Scorpius fought the urge to leap forward, sweep Lady Aerthrudha from her grandsire's reach and flee before it was too late.

The chancellor stepped forward slightly, grasping Scorpius by the elbow and pressing him closer to the rival dukes. "No trouble, Your Grace," the chancellor said. "We were discussing our duties, only."

Scorpius glanced sideways at the chancellor. *Duties.* What duty did he owe this house, other than to Lord Thibault, to whom he owed everything?

I never thought to help you search out your family when I brought you here, Lord Thibault had said on the stairs. *I just wanted you for my man.*

A cascade of memories assaulted him, filled with laughter, brotherly embrace, meeting blade with blade.

Razlava turned back to Pruzhnino, smiling the same hard smile he'd once used at the falconer's cottage. "Dutifully, I sent my granddaughter here, and dutifully I fetch her back again."

Lord Thibault's father nodded sadly. "Time seems so strangely to fly, does it not? Seems too short a time has gone by for this to be your granddaughter and not her aunt, your late daughter, the gods show their mercy."

Razlava took a tiny step backwards. Thrusting his chin forward, he said, "I thank you for your memories of her."

"Lady Aerthrudha is the spitting image of her, don't you think?" Pruzhnino said, stepping forward to grasp the maiden softly by the chin.

She gazed intently into Pruzhnino's eyes. "Do you think so?" she asked. "No one ever speaks of her. My aunt."

Scorpius' gut hollowed out inside him. He could barely get his breath.

"What could she have been, other than a beauty?" the chancellor said. "Seeds don't drift far, only far enough to bloom."

"Some seeds drift, my Lord Chancellor," Razlava said. "Some seeds only produce chaff." As he spoke, he stepped slowly toward Scorpius, looking him up and down.

"My dear," Pruzhnino said, cupping his palm gently on Lady Aerthrudha's cheek, "you may be sure your mother held every man under her spell. Including me."

"Would that my daughter had been your choice of bride then, Pruzhnino," Razlava said, stopping before Scorpius and gazing down in haunted distraction.

"Who could say if that would have saved her." Pruzhnino took the maiden's face in his hands and kissed the tears away.

97

"Is there a particular reason you've brought Lord Thibault's man here, rather than your son, himself?" Razlava said, turning to Pruzhnino.

"He'll provide escort to your retinue as you depart the duke's estate, Your Grace," the chancellor said.

Both Pruzhnino and the chancellor looked at Scorpius. The unspoken questions hung in the air like an arrow sprung from its bow but not yet landed. Would Scorpius reveal himself? Would Razlava claim a bastard grandson whose dark coloring spoke of scandal successfully hushed up for almost two decades?

Razlava bowed his head in acknowledgement of their dismissal. He stretched out his hand for his granddaughter's.

This was it. Scorpius must choose.

Somehow this moment felt like all the others, those blinks of an eye where everything in Scorpius' world had turned upside down. Why had he supposed that being given a choice would make any of it easier?

Turning swiftly to the chancellor, Scorpius knocked the advisor's hat to the side as he made his reverence. For one terrible moment the close-cropped Sibian hair revealed itself before the chancellor replaced the hat with shaking hands.

Scorpius bowed low before the chancellor, raising his head to lock gazes with the shaken man. Turning elegantly to direct his bow to Pruzhnino, he likewise gazed up at the duke to see something even more out of character than the sweet nothings he'd been saying to Lady Aerthrudha — fear.

Well, he'd seen fear — real fear — on the faces of those slaves chased and brought down upon the hunting field by this noble, who had never claimed his own daughter's child at the nursery all those years ago.

If Scorpius was really free to choose, how could he reach for a life that brought him into arms' length of this man? How could Pruzhnino and the chancellor ask him to do it?

"With respect, Your Grace, my Lord Chancellor — duty

calls. In fact I am sworn to protect my Lord Thibault, your son," he said, sweeping an arm towards Pruzhnino. "I shall find another of the duke's men to escort Your Grace and Lady Aerthrudha from the estate. One man is as good as the next, I'm sure you will find."

The chancellor found his voice. "Send the guard down to the stables. No need to keep His Grace and the lady waiting."

Bowing crisply, Scorpius said, "Certainly, my Lord Chancellor. Your Grace. Your Grace. My lady."

Striding from the drawing room, Scorpius took only a few steps before he broke into a run, taking stairs three at a time until he regained the ballroom. It only took a glance and he knew his master was not there.

Looking left and right, Scorpius forced himself to stillness, listening for Lord Thibault's telltale laugh. Wandering back to the staircase, he recalled his promise to send another in his place and dispatched a slave to the stables.

Suddenly he heard it. His master's unbridled delight in his Sibian bride-to-be carried down the corridor and over the gallery railings. Scorpius followed the sound until it brought him before the dukessa's door.

Lord Thibault turned and stared, his grin half-frozen on his face. Scorpius' heart chilled even in the warmth of the dukessa's drawing room at the thought of never seeing his master again.

Crossing the floor towards one another, Scorpius and Lord Thibault collided in the center of the room in a back-slapping embrace. When they released their hold, his master grabbed Scorpius by the face and kissed his forehead.

Scorpius fell to one knee and kissed Lord Thibault's hand. "I believe in you," he said. "In what you're doing. And I shall serve you, my lord."

Yashtii joined them, kneeling beside Scorpius to embrace him. The dukessa swept close and stood beside her son.

Then a member of Yashtii's kinsmen fell to his knees between Scorpius and his master's intended. Retrieving something from inside his tunic, he took Scorpius' hand and dropped the dukessa's dragon ring into his palm.

All the Sibiu gathered there drew around in a circle and began humming a mournful tune. Looking up into Yashtii's face, Scorpius watched her nod solemnly, a tiny hint of a smile tugging at one side of her mouth.

Offering it back to the dukessa, Scorpius knelt there with the hair on his neck stirring as though the breath of the dragon blew through the drawing room. Lord Thibault's mother took Scorpius' hand in hers, lifted the ring with delicate fingers and placed the ring back upon Scorpius' hand.

The Sibiu finished their song. His master bid him rise and join him as they waited for his father the duke to arrive to hammer out the marriage bargain.

Scorpius wished Lady Aerthrudha all the happiness in the world, truly.

Looking down upon the dragon ring, all at once the spectre of dragon's fire which had haunted him all of his life blackened and shriveled, floating away like so many embers. He placed his ringed hand on the pommel of his sword, gazing upon it, knowing for the first time what it truly meant to belong.

END OF BOOK ONE

Author Bio

Award-winning filmmaker and author Julia Phillips Smith lives on Canada's East Coast with her husband and her mom, where the rugged sea and misty forests feed her thirst for gothic tales.

A graduate of Ryerson University's film program, Julia's previous writing credits include scripts for radio and television, along with Book 1 of her Dark Ages vampire series.

A longtime blogger, she invites you to visit A Piece of My Mind (http://julia-mindovermatter.blogspot.com/).

www.ingramcontent.com/pod-product-compliance
Lightning Source LLC
Chambersburg PA
CBHW022039240626
47154CB00007B/2483